Ten Seconds 'til

A Seamus O'Connor Thriller

Braxton DeGarmo

Christen Haus Publishing

Copyright

Ten Seconds 'til – Copyright © 2017 by Braxton DeGarmo. All rights reserved under International and Pan-American Copyright Conventions. No part of this text may be reproduced, transmitted, down-loaded, decompiled, reverse engineered, or stored in or introduced into any information and retrieval system, in any form or by any means, whether electronic or mechanical, now known or hereinafter invented, without the express written permission of Braxton DeGarmo.

ISBN (paperback): 978-1-943509-30-0
ISBN (mobi): 978-1-943509-28-7
ISBN (ePub): 978-1-943509-29-4

Cover design by Rocking Book Covers

For more information, go to: **www.braxtondegarmo.com**

DEDICATION

This story is dedicated to first responders everywhere, who often place their lives at risk to maintain the safety of ours.

AUTHOR'S NOTE

For those of you who have never read my work, Sergeant Seamus O'Connor is the main character from my debut novel, *The Militant Genome*. I have had many requests for a sequel to that novel, as well as for a series based on his character and that of his kinda-sorta girlfriend, Sarah Wade, MD. Unfortunately, I already had my MedAir Series in the works with a different set of characters. So, I added Seamus to the storyline at the end of book two: *Rescued and Remembered*. Since then, he has been a re-occurring character in that series, as well as my go-to guy for novellas such as this one.

I hope you enjoy this story. It was fun researching explosives and bomb disposal techniques. So far, no police authorities have come knocking on my door to ask about my online search history.

One

This was not the place to be at night, they said. Black, white, red, yellow — no lives mattered here, if you listened to the press. Some considered it no-man's land even during the brightest hour of the day.

The police seldom ventured here and when they did, they regretted it. Not that they became targets, although that, too, happened on occasion—the random gunshot at a patrol car. Inevitably on patrol, they would come across someone else's target, dumped there for eventual discovery. Or not.

So, why in the world had "Susan" driven down this road? Sure, Google maps said this was the shortest and fastest path to an open gas station that now sat just a few blocks away, where the street opened onto the service road adjacent to the interstate. Couldn't she have made it there, or to a different station, using a different route? She could see the brightly lit facility not far away, with only one stop sign between it and her to slow her down. Should she ignore it? She saw no other headlights moving toward the intersection.

The question about stopping became a moot issue as her car coasted to a halt a hundred feet before the intersection. Also obvious was that, no, taking a different path would not have helped. She appeared to be out of gas.

The correct choice of a sane person would be to grab your cell phone and call for assistance. As a sign of her sanity, she decided that would take too long, even if she could convince AAA to come to her location. She looked into the distance at the bright lights that beckoned and knew she had one choice. How long would it take her, in heels, to get there?

She grabbed her purse and pulled a handgun from it. A 9mm Beretta. She tucked it into her coat pocket and exited the car. She set off at as fast a pace as she could comfortably handle without risking breaking a heel. As she passed the stop sign, the voices seemed to come from nowhere.

"Slow down there, mama. Wassup?"

"Yeah, baby. We gonna show you a good time."

She turned toward the voices to see three young men, in hoodies that hid their faces. Gloves covered their hands. She would guess them to be black, but then, she would never be able to testify to that. She couldn't see their faces between the hoodies and shadows. Definitely not white. Not in this part of town.

"Ple-please, don't hurt me. I-I ran out of gas. I just need to get a little to get it started and I'll be out of here."

Her voice choked as she began to speak. The rest of her sentence sounded raspy. One of the men cocked his head to scrutinize her. A second turned to look at the car. She doubted the twelve-year-old Camry interested them, especially being out of gas. That left two things of potential interest, her purse   . . . and her. She zipped her purse closed and felt it click.

The second man turned back and said, "Car's a piece a junk. But you lookin' good."

In the faint light, she could see an attempt at a smile, minus most of his teeth. The first man leaned over and said something into the man's ear. The smile faded.

"Ya think? Mighty C, why don'we check unda da hood and see whats we got here?"

As he stepped toward her, she pulled her gun from her pocket and pointed it toward them. They didn't seem fazed.

"D-don't come—"

The third man surprised her by grabbing her purse and ripping it off her shoulder. She was knocked off-balance, but she held on to the gun. She started to reissue her warning, but the trio began to laugh and took off running.

"We be back. Don't go far!" one of them yelled.

She saw them again about fifty yards away, walking, as they passed through the light cast off by a nearby billboard. They stopped at the base of the sign and, using its light, began to inspect the purse.

Oh, I doubt it, Mighty C, she thought as she smiled. The explosion toppled the billboard onto a work van parked nearby. She regretted the task that lay ahead for the city's Evidence Technician Unit (ETU).

At the same brisk walk, she returned to the car and retrieved the key from under the seat. She doffed the long, black wig and tossed it into the back seat before starting the car and driving off. She laughed as she made a turn at the stop sign. She didn't want anyone at the gas station seeing her drive past. Plus, she didn't want to drive through the crime scene. Tires tracking through blood could be matched.

She thought about "her" performance. Getting into character, finding the right attitude, and acting the part made her actions so much more convincing. Female tonight. Maybe a male persona the next time. Still, tonight's female made a mental note to work on the voice.

Two

Seamus O'Connor sat down at his kitchen table with some heated leftovers after a much-too-long day. He wondered what had been added to the water that now caused the craziness he witnessed each day. Gang slayings. Drive-by shootings, also gang related. Attacks on fellow officers. Kids shooting their siblings. Murder-suicides by raging ex-spouses.

What had happened to sanity? Where was all this leading society? Did the rule of law no longer mean anything?

He had expected the gangs to increase their attacks on each other. The shooting two years earlier of a young thug by an officer in a nearby community had set off days of riots and months of protests, all based upon the lies of a few "witnesses" whose self-interests were in conflict with the truth. The mainstream media had been eager to promote that lie and castigate the police. One of the many truths they hadn't reported was that the situation had produced a ripe field for recruiting by the gangs. New initiates, out to prove themselves worthy, now surfed a wave of shootings and homicides that once again made St. Louis one of the most dangerous cities in America. The rise of that wave into a tsunami was what surprised him.

Halfway into his meal, his cell phone rang.

"O'Connor."

"Shay, your services are requested up north on Bircher near Marcus."

Seamus sighed. Why didn't his lieutenant ever call with good news, like being awarded a medal for meritorious service, or that his March Madness bracket won the office pool?

"That's District Six. Why are they calling us?"

"Not them. The Chief has assigned you to a joint task force with the FBI. Apparently, they don't know any better and asked for you by name."

Seamus rolled his eyes at the gibe but thought about that for a moment. He'd been on joint task forces before. That meant this case was unusual. Seamus offered a half grin to the phone. He liked the challenge of the unusual.

"Okay. Do I have time to finish eating?"

"Sure. They'll be there *all* night."

Seamus frowned at the way his superior emphasized 'all.' He'd need to stop and get a strong cup of coffee on the way. He'd opt for a gallon, if someone would sell it in bulk.

Twenty-five minutes later, Seamus arrived on

scene from the west end of Bircher Boulevard but was stopped two blocks away by uniformed officers. He showed his police credentials, but that moved him no closer. He parked between two marked patrol cars and headed the rest of the way on foot. While still a block away, he saw his first evidence marker . . . next to a finger.

He looked ahead and saw the crumpled remains of someone's work truck, partially covered by the twisted mass of a fallen billboard. He couldn't make out the sign's message nor the company's name on the side of the truck. The truck appeared to be of the boom lift variety—a cherry picker, as some would call it. No businesses came to mind in the area that would require the lift, but then, this wasn't his precinct and he couldn't be expected to know it as well as his own.

As he progressed toward the main area of activity, the evidence tags and body parts became more prominent. He had counted three arms to that point, so he knew they had at least two victims. There might be more. He watched where he stepped.

"Took you long enough."

"Detective LaToya, que pasa?"

Having astutely surmised that they were dealing with some sort of bombing, Seamus felt no surprise at seeing Sergeant Denise LaToya at the scene. The slim woman, whose coal black hair seemed always pulled back into a ponytail, was all-business whenever they had crossed paths. No, in reflection, she came across as hard and unemotional, something of a loner. Perhaps she had been this way since childhood, but Seamus suspected that her time in the Middle East had left its mark on her psyche.

An ex-Army ordinance expert and member of the bomb squad, she knew more about the forensics of an explosion than most of the other metropolitan detectives combined, except maybe for one hard-headed senior tech of Polish descent. He had no doubt Joe Marcinkiewicz was somewhere on the scene. Still, from the pool of explosive forensics experts nationwide, *she* had been called in as an expert at the Boston Marathon bombing two years earlier.

"Just what it looks like. So far, we've identified three individuals. Well, not as in knowing who they were, just that three were involved. The point of detonation appears to have been right under the billboard." She held up an evidence bag holding what looked like imitation leather. Real leather would have appeared shredded, not torn, at the edges. "Taking this to my van for a quick test for residue. Has kind of a funky peppermint smell to it." She held it up to him to sniff. "Weird."

Seamus wondered whether he would even have thought to smell something like that to notice, but he nodded in agreement. "Where do I find the incident command?"

"Keep going down Bircher. Just past the downed billboard. You'll see the tables about a hundred yards beyond. I'll be there in a few minutes."

Seamus nodded and turned back to his original

course.

"Hey, O'Connor, good to see you."

Seamus turned at the voice to see Sergeant AJ Darst of the Evidence Technician Unit, the city's version of CSI. The man held an expensive camera in his hands.

"You, too, AJ. What are you doing here? The FBI has its own crime scene techs."

"Yeah, they needed more eyes and hands, so a few of us got called to the task force, too. I think they're also going to use our lab for some of their testing. The hard stuff will go to the FBI labs, but they're backlogged almost as much as we are."

Seamus nodded and pointed to the camera. "So, what . . . they got you taking still lifes or just glamour shots of LaToya there?"

Surprised that she responded, he grinned as LaToya shouted back, "I heard that."

"Doing the video walk-through of the scene. I'd need a special camera to shoot LaToya."

Both men grinned as she shouted, "Idiots! I heard that, too. Keep it up and you'll need to check your cars before starting them."

He glanced at the woman. A sense of humor? Sort of. Maybe Seamus didn't know the woman as well as he thought. He turned back to the ETU sergeant.

"Is your team out in force with the bomb squad?"

Darst nodded. "Yeah. We called everyone in that we could, because of the size of the scene. I've been working on this video for over 30 minutes. I've covered so much territory, I feel like I'm doing a travelogue for a small country."

Seamus chuckled. "Well, I better find the command center and get to work then. See you around."

"Yeah. Hey, let's get together for a beer sometime."

"Sure." He gave the ETU sergeant a thumb up.

As stated, the command center was beyond the billboard. He could see it now. He passed a BP station which sat across from the lot holding the billboard, which he now saw advertised a bank. That lot, on the east side of Marcus Avenue, held an automotive repair company. Maybe the cherry picker was there for repairs. Too late for that now.

The St. Louis Regional Bomb & Arson Unit was out in force, from what Seamus saw as he approached the command tables. Two years earlier, the city and county had merged their bomb squads into one unit. The results had been good for the area, and a cost-saver for both police departments. The unit now had the latest "toys" and the price tag had been split between the two sets of bean counters.

" 'Bout time you showed up," quipped Frank DeLeo. Seamus had worked a few times before with the five-foot-six FBI agent. "The other guys are out helping locate and tag body parts." Most of those "other guys" called DeLeo "Napoleon." Some had a name for him that was a less than flattering play on the name. Behind his back, of course.

Seamus shrugged. "Got here as soon as I could." He grabbed a stack of evidence markers and turned to join the others.

"Not so fast, baby face. I have a different task for you."

Seamus closed his eyes and counted to ten. It might be true that his Irish roots had given him a pale complexion, red hair, and a face that hadn't aged much for the past fifteen years. Yet, at age 31, his five-foot-ten-inch frame had fifty pounds of muscle over DeLeo, and he'd been working homicides for nearly five years now, compared to Napoleon's two with the agency. He had learned to control his Irish anger about fifteen years earlier as well, but there were times.

He was about to turn back to the short man and say something less than complimentary, but the Special Agent-in-Charge walked up. S-A-C Randolph Redmond was an old-school, feet-on-the-ground kind of investigator who begrudgingly accepted today's technology. The older man grabbed the evidence markers from Seamus and shoved them into DeLeo's hands.

"Go help find and mark anything that looks like evidence. *I've* got a different task for O'Connor."

Napoleon looked insulted but stepped from behind the table and set off toward the billboard. Seamus let about half of the smile he felt inside show on his face.

"I hear he's being his usual pain in the . . ." The S-A-C paused. "Well, that should keep him busy. Anyway, Welch should be here in a moment."

Detective Brian Welch was with the Sixth District. This was his home turf. They'd met, but Seamus didn't know him well. At least he had a reputation of being easygoing and playing well with others.

"Looks like we might have IDs from two of the victims." The man held up two clear plastic evidence bags. Each held a bloody driver's license. "These were fished from the back pockets of shredded jeans. Actually, that's overstating the condition of those jeans. If these guys were up to no good, I'm hoping Welch might know them."

"Who might I know? Hey, O'Connor, good to see you again." He peeled off his pair of bloody vinyl gloves, tossed them into a trash receptacle next to the closest table, and extended his hand in greeting.

"Welch. You, too." Seamus accepted his handshake.

S-A-C Redmond held out the evidence bags. Welch scrutinized the IDs. He nodded.

"Yeah, I know these two. A couple of gangbangers—with the Crips. Each one has a lengthy rap sheet for B&E, assault, and burglary. Both have served some hard time." He shook his head. "Never heard of them being involved with explosives. That would be a big step for them." He appeared to be thinking about that possibility. "I'll ask around about the bomb aspect. But, if these two are dead, our third guy is probably Seymour Hutchins, a.k.a. 'Mighty C.' He's the older brother of this one." He held up one of the two bags to show that ID. "Now, him? Yeah, I could see him graduating from Explosives 101. Bad as they come. He was convicted of second-degree murder a few months ago, and had the conviction overturned on a technicality. A new trial date was set and the prosecution's lead witness disappeared. Nada. No trace."

"Hey! Whadda we got here?"

Seamus turned toward the gravelly voice. Marcinkiewicz.

"We don't need you guys. We got this scene covered."

Seamus knew better than to take the old Pole's tough talk to heart. He could see the gleam in the detective's eye, a telltale sign the man was goading them. Likewise, he could tell Redmond didn't know the man, much less that he was jesting. He spoke up before the S-A-C.

"Q-wicz, you might have the scene covered, but we're here to *solve* the case."

The bomb tech's face broke into a broad smile. "Shay, good to see you. Who you got with you?" He nodded toward the other two men.

Seamus made the introductions, just as Sgt. LaToya walked up to be included.

"So, a joint task force?" asked Marcinkiewicz. "We don't need the extra bodies."

"Your chief demanded it," replied the agent. "Otherwise, we can claim total jurisdiction on this one."

LaToya nodded. "And I think the chief is right on this one. Same guy, Q-wicz."

The older detective shook his head as something that sounded like "shhhi ..." escaped his lips but didn't finish.

Seamus wondered. "Same guy? What's that mean?" He hadn't heard of any other bomb incidents, much less any with injuries.

Q-wicz spoke up. "Someone's been blowing up street-side trash cans. Nothing major, and no collateral damage, but we couldn't ID the explosive. Had its own peculiar odor, though."

"Yeah, that's why I think this is the same guy."

Seamus shook his head. If that was true, the trash cans were just practice. And the practice swings were finished.

Three

❧◆◆❧

"Harry" had told everyone within earshot that the bar on Laclede's Landing, after an evening in the casino, was a great place to celebrate one's winnings, starting with a round for everyone. He soon realized, though, that he had attracted interest of a different sort, less concerned about having a good time at his expense.

He glanced down along the bar and saw the man watching. As he caught the man's eyes with his own, the man would divert his stare to someplace else in the room, only to return his gaze back when the man thought he wasn't looking. The normal person would feel uncomfortable with the undue attention.

After his third drink, he stretched and stated, "Well, folks, it's been a blast partying with you, but it's time to head home, get a good night's sleep."

He could feel the bulge of his overstuffed wallet in his back pants pocket. But, instead of retrieving it, he pulled a small wad of cash from his jacket's inner pocket.

"Barkeep!" He raised his hand toward the woman making drinks with the dexterity of a juggler. He paid his tab, and for a second time, said his goodbyes to the strangers who had joined him.

Once outside, he picked up his pace and headed toward his car. At the first intersection, he decided to turn down the smaller alley as a shortcut back to the parking lot. He glanced behind him and saw no one. He figured he was safe. He had only been imagining the worst back in the bar.

Still, he saw no reason to dilly-dally. He made a beeline straight down the middle of the road. Well, if the bee had been as drunk as he felt. The straight line looked more like a sine wave.

He was 20 feet from the light of the next intersection when he heard a voice.

"Stop right there and put ya hands wheres I can see 'em."

He complied. In the next instant, he saw the man from the bar. He looked bigger now. Maybe six-foot-one and beefier, maybe 230. He was no match for this man.

"Now. With one hand, fetch that money of yours and give it to me."

"Please. Don't hurt me. I-I'll give you the money."

The man didn't appear to have a gun and he flashed no knife. He thought maybe he could toss the cash and run, get clean away. Otherwise, well, he didn't relish a beating . . . or worse if the guy produced a weapon.

He slowly moved his right hand and started to

reach into his jacket's inside pocket.

'Nuh-uh. Not that. I wants the wallet in ya back pocket. Reach for it slow like. If I sees you go for a gun unda da coat, you won't make it out a here in one piece."

He raised his right hand again and slowly reached into his left rear pocket with his left. He gently pulled the fat wallet from his pants. At that point, another man emerged from the shadows, pointing a handgun at him.

"H-here." He slowly handed the wallet toward the first man, his hand trembling. At the last moment, he dropped it. As both men watched it drop to the pavement, he bolted. This time there was no weave to his direction.

As he rounded the corner, he heard the two men laughing. He stopped and resumed a normal walk toward the parking lot. Two seconds later, the blast shook the buildings around him. They obviously had opened the wallet wide enough—first, to see that it held no cash and second, to trigger the simple detonator.

As he climbed into his beat-up Camry, he heard the approaching sirens. Upon exiting the lot, he turned and went the opposite direction. In reflection, "his" male persona had been easier to pull off. Still, he had other characters he wished to try. And other thugs he wished to fry. He liked the sound of that. Maybe he'd make that his motto.

And then, proudly he thought, "Gee, only two outings and I'm an ace. Five scumbags down, lots more to go." He smiled as he passed a speeding patrol car heading the other way.

Four

❧ ◆ ◆ ☙

Seamus looked up from his computer as he heard the report on the scanner. An explosion, with casualties, on Laclede's Landing. He expected his phone to ring at any moment.

Until it did, he continued the research he had started online. Alfred Nobel. The inventor of dynamite, gelignite, and the blasting cap. Founder of ninety armament factories. Holder of 350 patents. And a man whose fortune was left to a foundation that honors the best achievements of man, including the Nobel Peace Prize. What an enigmatic individual.

One of those inventions was Nobel 808, the original plastique, or as it's now called, plastic explosive. C4 and Semtex are the common modern forms, and according to Sgt. LaToya, no one uses Nobel 808. No one until now, maybe.

His cell phone rang. "O'Connor."

"Shay, it's LaToya. We have another one."

"Yeah, I heard the call come across the scanner.

Are you there already?" Fifteen minutes hadn't passed since he heard the call.

"Believe it or not, I was just around the corner. Felt the blast."

Seamus pondered that for a moment.

"Did you see anyone? Are you sure it's the same guy?"

"If you mean, did I see anyone running away from the scene, sure, at least three dozen people. We had total chaos for about five minutes. As for being the same guy, let's just say the scene smells like peppermint. You figure out the odds."

Seamus sat back in his chair. From his discussions with LaToya and Q-wicz, plus his online search, he'd learned that some form of oil was used to help keep plastic explosives soft and pliable. For C4, the recipe called for a dash of motor oil. For Nobel 808, they could only speculate that Nobel had used almond oil, which would have given its reputed almond scent. The problem was that the chemical composition of Nobel 808 seemed as secretive as the recipe for Coca-Cola or the spices used in Colonel Sanders' fried chicken. He could find it nowhere on the web. Even the bomb squad could only guess at its actual makeup.

Apparently, their perp in these cases used peppermint oil. Maybe that could be called his signature.

"I'll be there in ten minutes."

Seamus passed through the police cordon and

found LaToya at the incident command center. She glanced at her cell phone upon noticing him.

"Hey, that's pretty good. Ten minutes on the nose, give or take a few seconds."

"I strive to be punctual." He glanced around the scene. "Anyone else here from the task force?"

"Not that I've seen."

"So, what've we got?"

Sgt. LaToya stepped away from the command center and pointed to a white shroud near the sidewalk about fifty feet away, toward the Mississippi River. "Two dead. They must have been holding the device at about waist level. Severe chest and abdominal trauma. One guy's arms blown off, but not like the previous scene. We don't have body parts scattered over the block."

"Have you determined the explosive?"

She shook her head. "I was down here with family, not the bomb squad. I'm waiting on the equipment. It shouldn't be long."

Seamus noticed a uniformed officer approaching them. Behind him, at the police line, a woman rocked back and forth on her feet, her arms crossed in front of her chest. She would stop moving, run a hand through her hair, and then cross her arms and begin to rock again. Seamus guessed that she might have information for them.

"Detectives," said the officer. "We have a witness to the event over there. Do you want me to take her statement?"

Seamus liked the officer's willingness, but this would best be left for him to do.

"I'll handle it. Tell her I'll be with her in a moment. Thanks."

As the officer moved back toward the woman, LaToya said, "I'll join you. Can't do anything else until my equipment gets here."

"Sure, c'mon."

Seamus saw the Evidence Technician Unit van pull up to and then enter the police cordon at the other end of the street. One of the ETU officers climbed down from the driver's seat. A moment later, she was joined by Sergeant Darst who walked out from behind the corner building. They appeared set to work and hadn't noticed Seamus and LaToya.

They found the witness, and after introductions, Seamus escorted the woman into the police cordon and off to the side where they could speak privately. She appeared to be late thirties, five-foot-five, and maybe one-fifty. She wore a uniform top that labeled her as an employee of a local restaurant.

"So, Ms. Henderson, you told the officer that you saw what happened."

"That's right. I had finished my shift at work and was heading for my car. Two guys were following what looked like a lone man who turned from up there. I say man because of the way he walked, kinda drunk, but more like a guy. He was kind of short. I couldn't see a face or hair or anything. Anyway, the person started up there..." She turned and pointed toward 2nd Street. "..

. and headed this way. The two men ran down that alley to get ahead of him. As the guy passed the other end of the alley, the bigger of the two guys stepped out and confronted him. Looked like a robbery, so I stopped dead in my tracks. The second guy came out of the shadows and held a gun. I was about to turn the other way and go call for help, when I saw the victim pull out his wallet and drop it. The two men kept watching the wallet as it fell and the victim took off running. The bigger man picked up the wallet and it looked like it exploded in his hands as he tried to open it. That's when I took off running, too."

Seamus questioned her comment about going to call for help, but maybe this lady was an exception. Most people would turn away and refuse to get involved.

"Could you identify any of the men?"

She shook her head. "Sorry. I didn't see any faces. They were all in front of me."

Plus, it was dark and streetlights cast only so-so light while creating a lot of shadows. Seamus knew he wouldn't get anything more useful from her. "Well, thanks. Let me get some contact information from you in case we have any other questions."

Concluding that, they let her leave and together walked back toward the center of the scene.

LaToya spoke up first. "Well, sure sounds like this guy, the one they tried to rob, was out to take care of some bad guys, just like the scene from the other night. From what we've pieced together, that incident used a woman's purse to hold the explosive. We also found what appears to be the remnants of a detonator. Still trying to figure it out."

Seamus thought about that for a moment and nodded. "That would fit. More explosive, bigger, messier scene. Still, you'd want to guarantee being further from the explosion before it goes off. Less explosive, less damage to the victims. You might not find the same kind of detonator because the perp wouldn't have to be farther away."

"Good point. We need to look for the remains of a wallet." LaToya pointed to their right. "Hey, my stuff just arrived. Let's see what we can find. With some luck, I'll have something to test."

As they neared the covered bodies, the techs from the medical examiner's office waved them over.

"Detectives, come closer."

They did. Seamus had been to some gruesome crime scenes in his day, but this one was worse than the last one. There, he had to witness various body parts. Here, he would get an anatomy lesson of the human thorax and abdomen.

But, the tech surprised him and didn't uncover the bodies.

"Cause of death is obvious. Don't need to belabor that. I called you over for one reason. What do you smell?"

Seamus took a cautious whiff of the air. LaToya had been right. Peppermint.

Seamus worked the police line looking for other

witnesses. He was joined by his "favorite" agent, DeLeo, whom he tried to avoid by working the other end of the line. Yet, the guy kept drifting back toward Seamus.

"Hey, Frank, I got these folks covered. No witnesses. Did you finish canvassing the other side?"

The man's lips formed a snarl. "Whadda you think? Of course, I did."

"Any other witnesses?"

The man shook his head. "No. Just curious gawkers."

Seamus glanced at the man. The guy looked angrier than usual, or maybe the scowl was permanent.

He left the man behind to survey new onlookers and took his next cue from their one witness. The bomber appeared to be male, drunk, and walking from 2nd Street. The casino had its own parking, so Seamus thought it unlikely that he'd been drinking at one of the bars there. That left about half-a-dozen restaurants and bars between his current location and the casino. Time for some old-fashioned, pound-the-pavement, detective work.

He walked back to the victims and approached the medical examiner's crew.

"Can I get a picture of their faces? I want to check out the local bars and see if anyone saw them."

The lead tech grimaced. "I'd like to help there, but these faces wouldn't be recognized by their mothers."

"What about IDs? Did you find driver's licenses or any other ID on them?"

The woman nodded. "Ummm, the M.E. doesn't like

us to release evidence at the scene."

Seamus knew that. Anything and everything found on a body fell under their jurisdiction until released by the M.E. But that didn't stop him from taking a picture of such evidence. He pulled out his cell phone.

"So, you *did* find IDs, right? Let me take a picture of them."

The two techs looked at each other, uncertain about his request.

"The M.E. doesn't like us to release anything until we have positive ID. Since I can't compare the face to the ID, I'm not sure I —"

Seamus took a deep breath. "Look. I get it. Maybe he robbed someone else tonight and held on to the guy's ID as a souvenir, but . . ." He hoped he didn't sound too sarcastic. ". . . right now that's all I have to work with. Let's go with the odds and expect this to be the correct ID."

The look on the woman's face confirmed he had come across as sarcastic, or maybe just patronizing. Still, she went to their van and returned with two clear evidence bags, which she held out to him.

He took a look at the first bag, and then the second. He shook his head. He recognized both men . . . more from their rap sheets than personal experience. The younger, "Birdshot" Browning, was a two-bit thug who typically affiliated with someone bigger and more experienced. More like a strong-armed robber's wingman.

This time he'd picked the wrong guy, a career

criminal who was as likely to take out his accomplice as much as any victim. Victor Cochran took his first name seriously. He hated coming in second place, and yet, he'd spent more years behind bars at the correctional center in Bonne Terre, Missouri, than outside those bars. Curiously, Victor had something in common with Seymour Hutchins. He'd recently beaten a charge that could have led to a lifetime supply of orange jumpsuits and a room with his number on it—saved not by innocence or crafty attorneys, but by a technicality.

Two cases did not create a pattern, but could they have some vigilante on the loose?

Seamus took photos of the two drivers licenses and handed them back to the tech. As he did so, he recalled something else about Cochran.

"The big guy there. Is there enough of his left upper arm to see if he has a big scar on it?"

The woman nodded. "There is and he does. Looks like something took a chunk of his arm out in the past. A bullet maybe."

"Yeah. That's exactly what did it, and I'm confident you'll get your positive ID on these two. The officer who shot him retired last month. I'll let him know."

Five

❦◆◆❧

"He" glanced at his image in the mirror and combed back the salt-and-pepper hair that fringed his head below the tanned pate that crowned him. With the addition of a bushy, gray mustache and glasses, he looked many years older than his real age, not to mention much more financially successful. He nodded in satisfaction over this latest addition to his character "wardrobe."

He slid on a sports jacket, picked up a leather briefcase—also to add to the look of success—and headed for his garage. He climbed into the old Camry and headed off toward his workshop, located in an old warehouse not far away. There, he pulled the car inside and closed the door.

It had been a week since the Laclede Landing success—two more criminals off the streets. He was eager to resume but had needed time, both to let the local police vigilance calm down and to finish his pet project. This one had taken months to plan, equip, and put together. More time had been needed to acquire his target and gather intelligence on his routines, favorite hangouts, likes, and dislikes.

The target loved cars—mostly those that weren't his. He was believed to be responsible for more than one hundred auto thefts over the previous five years, but only one theft charge had been brought against him successfully—until a technicality threw that case out of court. However, more infuriating was that the man's thefts had also resulted in nearly a dozen vehicular manslaughters—allegedly. With no proof that he'd stolen the cars in the first place, authorities had no way of pinning him with those deaths.

The man's second vice appeared to be busty blondes in short skirts. That costume and character alone had taken "Heather" weeks to perfect, to get just the right amount of bimbo into the act. It had required confiding about "that time of the month" to keep his wandering hands from straying too far. Yet, "Heather" had succeeded in drawing out the man's boasts, in gaining confirmation that he could take any car he desired and not get caught, and in securing his promise to take her for a ride in her "dream car"—a Lamborghini—should he come across one.

As "Edward," he was about to further the target's lust.

He opened another set of wide doors within the warehouse and walked into that space, which clearly held a vehicle hidden beneath a white dust cover. He pulled the cloth away to reveal a very convincing knockoff of the 'one-off' Lamborghini Centenario Roadster. Built over a VW frame and engine, the fiberglass body had been fashioned by an expert. Even the interior looked authentic, until you tried to use the center console and realized it was only a prop.

What wouldn't be seen was the explosive charge under the driver's seat, built into a chamber that would direct all of the force upward. A passenger would be bloodied, but uninjured—if his calculations were correct. Unfortunately, he couldn't afford testing those calculations.

This project had set him back more than all of his others combined. This thief, after all, had been the prime motivator for vigilante justice. The others were simply practice. *This* man had stolen more than a car from "Edward."

But, that explosive charge had yet to be installed. This evening's foray was one designed to set the trap, to display the bait.

Six

❧✦✦☙

"Agent Redmond, you asked to meet with me?"

Seamus knocked on the doorpost to S-A-C Redmond's office at the St. Louis FBI field office. The agent stood to greet Seamus. "Thanks for driving over. C'mon in and have a seat."

The man closed the door behind them and returned to his desk.

"So, what's up? I take it you got my last report. I have nothing new to add at this point."

Seamus didn't understand the need for a closed-door meeting. They could have discussed the case over the phone.

S-A-C Redmond nodded. "What's up is that I got a call from the head of the city's Criminal Investigation Division. He has a concern, one that I don't feel we should discuss over the phone."

Seamus had his concerns, too. He wondered if they ran in line with those of his CID chief.

"And that is?"

"He's worried that this serial bomber is one of yours."

Seamus nodded. Yes, their concerns did match. Too often, with serial arsonists, for example, the perpetrator was, say, a volunteer fireman. What were the odds that a serial bomber had the knowledge and expertise of a bomb squad member? Unless they were looking for someone with military demolitions training. And who else, outside the police, had knowledge of court records and who beat the system on technicalities? Sure, anyone who closely followed the city's or county's trials might know which criminals had their cases dismissed. But knowing *why* charges were dismissed required a deeper level of access and understanding.

"I can understand that concern, sir. But, we have a few problems there. The first case involved a woman's purse, while the second, a man's wallet. If we're looking for a woman, we have one choice. A man? We have several. And no matter which gender, we're looking for someone with excellent acting skills, able to cross genders and portray either one." One other thought crossed his mind. "Or . . . we have a team with both genders involved."

The S-A-C glanced away, looking thoughtful. "Good points. We need to take a closer look at everyone's backgrounds. We also need to look for any members of the military with demolitions training who might reside in the area now. I'll get one of the other guys to look into that aspect. I want you taking a close look at the bomb squad members." He paused as his countenance became somber. "Actually, *I'll* run the background check on the squad members while you deal with them individually and as a team. Let's keep that part of this investigation between you and me."

Seven

"Mildred" put the last of the bobby pins into her silver locks to hold her bun together. Satisfied that her hair would remain in place, she daubed a bit of mascara onto her upper eyelashes and overdid the blush and lipstick—like so many octogenarians with shaky hands might do. She added a dated pair of glasses and checked her image in the mirror. Drab housedress with slightly tattered cardigan sweater. A chain for the glasses. Large, old-tech hearing aids. Clunky orthopedic shoes and opaque stockings.

She nodded in approval. "That should work."

Staring back was an older version of Dana Carvey's "The Church Lady." In fact, many of the characters "she," or "he," portrayed had been inspired by the stand-up comedian. Although the critics had panned it, *The Master of Disguise*, the 2002 movie written by Carvey, had been a favorite. The idea of becoming someone else held great appeal, not that real life was boring. Despite long stretches of the mundane, those occasional episodes of wet-your-pants terror—while facing a device that might splatter you across the face of the earth—kept life interesting.

Mildred picked up a four-legged cane and added a stoop to her walk. Her "purse" came next. Although it looked as if she had stuffed it with everything important in her life, that was the usual subterfuge, as it had been with the overstuffed wallet for the Laclede operation. She made a point of keeping the zippered top only half closed. Fully closing the zipper would bring two contact points together, and after that moment, breaking the contact by unzipping the top would unleash her "justice."

"Would you like some help with that, ma'am? I can get someone to carry that to your car for you." The cashier smiled as she handed Mildred her change.

Mildred returned the facial gesture and shook her head. "That's okay, sweetie. It's just bread, milk, and a little cheese. I can manage. I don't like to be a bother."

With that she looped the handles of the two grocery bags over the handle of her cane, allowing them to dangle on each side of it. She feigned using a little more effort to move her cane.

"It's not a bother at all. Let me get someone to help."

Mildred waved off the young woman. "Thank

you, but that's not necessary."

She needed to remain a "target." The presence of a stock person or any other store employee would ruin that.

"Well, at least let me get you a cart. That'll make it easier for you." The woman left her post and returned a moment later with an empty cart. She took the two bags and placed them into the cart. She laid the cane across the opened child's seat. "There. You can put your purse there and use the cart to support you as you walk to your car."

Mildred smiled. "Thank you, dear."

In reality, this would work even better. A purse would be much easier to snatch from the cart than from around her shoulder.

She shuffled her way to the car, stopping halfway there as if to catch her breath. She scanned the area around her. People of all ages, sizes, and colors dotted the parking lot. She looked for a pair of men who would look out of place. She also looked to make sure no police cars were present. This lot had become the "workplace" for a couple of thugs who targeted elderly women and their purses. Word was they had met in prison and teamed up after being released. *Early* release, for both of them, despite pleas from their victims that their full sentences be completed.

Mildred noticed a car at the far end of the parking lot. The vehicle seemed poised for a quick getaway, unlike the employees' cars which were parked in a cluster at the other side of the lot. A moment later, a single male emerged from the passenger's side. She couldn't see if a driver remained with the car but noticed that the man had sidled between parked cars to get to the lane where she walked and now approached her. She zipped the purse closed.

Showtime! she thought.

As she reached for the trunk of her car—as more of a delay tactic than a need to place two small bags in it—the man closed the gap between them, pushed the cart into her, knocking her to the ground—performed by her for show—and grabbed her purse. He began to sprint back to his vehicle, which she saw had already begun to move toward the exit.

"Hey! Stop! Thief!"

Surprised by the male voice, she turned around to see a young man yelling after the purse snatcher and beginning to run after him. Mildred had no desire to see a bystander injured, particularly someone willing to come to the aid of an elderly victim. She used her cart, as if trying to get up from the ground, and pushed it into the do-gooder's path. He stumbled as it hit him.

She kept in character, using the bumper of her car to stand, and watched the thief enter the waiting vehicle. Seconds later, the entire car erupted in a ball of flame.

As everyone in the parking lot stopped and gazed at the burning car, she dashed to her door, climbed into the car, and within a moment pulled forward through the empty slot in front of her. As she pulled out of the lot and onto the main street, she heard sirens approaching.

Seamus recalled the time when the City of St. Louis fought hard to convince the grocery chains to open stores within the city. Only one major chain had responded, while a discount chain had recently started opening stores within underserved neighborhoods. The city still fought for more stores and didn't need scenes like the one he saw now at the parking lot not far from his own home. This was *his* turf. No need to call him through any task force.

Reminiscent of the first bombing's crime scene, a large area had been cordoned off. The burnt shell of a car—make and model indiscernible—sat at the far end, along with a badly damaged Chrysler Imperial nearby. Remarkably, he saw no other damage to cars or buildings, and he'd been told in route that there were no casualties other than the two individuals in the car.

A line of people stood at the police tape. The bomb squad's van sat to one side of the scene. Q-wicz saw him and waved. Seamus glanced around for others on the squad and made note of who wasn't there. LaToya emerged from behind the wreckage. Dan Schaeffer, another detective on the Bomb & Arson Unit, climbed down from the back of their van. Seamus made a mental note to check the duty roster for the unit, but he suspected these three would be the only ones here.

"O'Connor, over here!"

Seamus wasn't surprised to see S-A-C Redmond at the scene. The FBI would have been among the first to be called if the bomb squad suspected involvement of the serial bomber.

"Agent Redmond," he said in greeting. "Was the task force called? I got this call through dispatch."

Redmond shook his head. "No. I was called by Q-wicz and I was waiting to decide on calling the task force. Plus, I knew you'd be called in. I can help interview folks if you want, or I can work with the squad. One way or the other, let's touch base before leaving."

Seamus nodded. "I'll cover the potential witnesses . . . in case we need to follow up with any of them. My partner should be here shortly, too. Why don't you see what Q-wicz and the others on the unit have found? You might find that more interesting, but I don't expect any surprises."

"Fair enough." The S-A-C headed toward the bomb squad's van.

Seamus approached the closest uniformed officer at the police line. "Hey, Howie, what's up? Are all these people witnesses?" He nodded toward the bystanders.

"O'Connor." The officer nodded in acknowledgment. He pointed toward one end of the line. "Those ten claim to have witnessed it, but I think you'll find the guy over there, sitting on the curb, most helpful. His name's Walt Rayford. Age 35. Shops here regularly and knows a lot of the locals."

"Thanks." *Might as well cut to the chase*, he thought, as he walked to meet his prime witness, per Howie. "Mr. Rayford, I'm Sergeant O'Connor, one of the district detectives."

The man stood and extended his hand. "Nice to meet ya."

"Thanks for waiting. I know you probably want to get home."

The man offered a wan smile. "Trust me, this is a lot more exciting than what I have waiting for me there. I saw the whole thing. The old lady. The guy snatching her purse and running. The car exploding."

The mention of a purse-snatching caught Seamus' attention. "Tell you what, start at the beginning. And, if you don't mind, I'd like to record this."

The man shrugged. "Sure. Tell me when you're ready."

Seamus prepared his digital recorder and introduced the session with date, time, location, and the witness' name. He nodded at Rayford to start.

"Well, I shop here all the time. I just live a few blocks away. Anyway, we've had some problems here with thieves breaking into cars, taking purses, and the like. So, when I come outta the store, I was being more careful. I followed this old lady out. She was about this tall . . ." He used his hand to give her height. ". . . and walked really slow. As soon as I could I kinda buzzed past her and headed to my car. But as I put things in my trunk, she walked past me to her car. Her movement caught my eye and I looked up. That's when I seen this guy walking from over there . . . " He pointed to the burnt car. ". . . toward her. Something seemed up with him, so . . ." He continued his story through to the explosion and aftermath.

"So, you say you saw the guy take the purse from the cart and push the lady down with the cart. But, you gave me a funny look as you said that."

The man nodded. "Yeah. At first, I thought . . . that mean SOB, not only taking her purse but pushing her to the ground, too. Like, what was she going to do? Chase him? But the more I've replayed it in my head, the more I realize something was off about that. I mean, it looked like he pushed her down, but he didn't. She actually stopped the cart and for like a second seemed unfazed by it. Then she plopped down on her butt on her own to make it look like he'd pushed her down."

"Anything else?"

"Yeah. She probably saved my life. I started to yell and run after the thief. All of a sudden, I'm tripping over her cart. If that hadn't happened, I would have been in range of the explosion."

Seamus scrutinized his face. "You're giving me that same strange look."

"Again, something not quite right about it. I mean, I could see her trying to use it to help stand up and accidentally pushing it right in my way. But thinking about it more, the trajectory don't add up. Using the cart to stand up and pushing it away would have sent it this way." He demonstrated with his hands. "But, I was coming this way . . . " Again, his fingers did the running.   ". . . and she pushed it perfectly into my path."

Seamus now saw a bit of nobility in their unknown subject—their unsub. Yes, he, or she, was outside the law and merciless against 'his' victims. And yet, 'she' went out of her way to protect an innocent bystander.

"So, where's this lady now?"

The man slowly shook his head. "Got me. The explosion caught everyone's attention and when I looked for her, she and her car were gone."

"Gone? And you didn't notice her pulling out? From what you describe, she would have practically run into you as she backed out of the slot."

He appeared a bit flustered at that question. "You'd think, right? But she didn't back out. She *would* have hit me. So, she had to have pulled straight forward. And then I remembered thinking to myself when I first pulled into my slot that someone didn't know how to park a car. A car over there was parked all screwy, made it so no one could park in the two slots right in front of them. I remember thinking it was either some old person who shouldn't be on the road anymore, or a drunk. It wasn't until I looked for her again that I realized it was her car. And she was *really* old. I'm surprised she still has a license."

Seamus debated asking the two questions that first

came to mind. Was he sure she was old? Was he sure she was a she? But he didn't want to stir up a mess he couldn't clean up. The last thing they needed was a leak to the press about some potential 'master of disguise' bomber.

Instead, he asked, "Did you happen to get the license plate number, or a part of it?"

Rayford shook his head. "Sorry, everything happened too fast. I didn't even think of it until just before you came."

Seamus completed his last witness interview. Howie had been correct—Walt Rayford was by far the most helpful. Another man and a woman corroborated his story about a man running toward the car with something in his hands, but they couldn't say what it was. To others, their idea of being a witness was that the explosion caught their attention, and they looked up in time to see the fireball rising from the car.

As he thanked the woman he'd been talking with, he saw S-A-C Redmond standing nearby, waiting for him. He tucked his notepad and digital recorder into his jacket and walked over to the special agent.

"So, no surprises, right?"

The S-A-C nodded. "Got the complete rundown from Marcinkiewicz. The bomb residue tested the same as the others, but there isn't anything else to tie it to the other two bombings.

The addition of the car's gas tank exploding and the intense fire seems to have eliminated evidence of the bomb itself, but they're still looking."

"Peppermint smell?"

The agent shook his head. "Not this time, but again, the gasoline explosion could have taken care of that."

That made sense to Seamus. The explosive residue being a match was enough, along with the purse-snatching M.O. He shared that info with Redmond.

"I'm going to check the bomb squad duty roster when I get back to my desk," he added.

"Probably no need. Marcinkiewicz said the three of them were on duty and there were no changes to their schedules. However, . . ." He stressed the word. ". . . he also said that LaToya was on her way back from the crime lab and they had to wait 15 minutes for her."

Seamus nodded. "Okay. Guess I'll head to the lab and nose around. See if anyone confirms she was there when she got the call. I'll keep you posted."

Seamus didn't like snooping around on "their own." He understood the CID chief's concern, and the man's point was a valid one. Going back to the firefighter-arsonist scenario, those guys always seemed to show up at their own fires to help put them out. The bomb squad team assembled here had also been at both previous bombings. In fact, LaToya had been in the vicinity of the Laclede Landing incident.

He just couldn't buy into that. LaToya was internationally recognized. Marcinkiewicz he'd known for years. Schaeffer and two of the others were good detectives, but to his knowledge, had been accepted onto the squad because of interest, not exceptional backgrounds in ordinance, chemistry, or demolitions. None of the three had military backgrounds. Schaeffer, in particular, had only advanced to using the disposal trailer. He had yet to disarm a live device. Seamus couldn't see him building a device . . . any device, much less one as sophisticated as what they were encountering. He hoped the others on the task force had come up with some disgruntled vet as a suspect, so they could clear the squad.

"Hey, you wanna help or you just gonna stand there pondering the clouds?"

Q-wicz stood about 30 feet away, on the other side of the police tape. Seamus had to work to act normally around the squad now—another reason he wanted to clear the members.

Seamus walked toward the man. A taunting smile crossed his lips as he said, "You need help? I thought you told me you don't need us guys, that you got the scene covered."

"Yeah, well—this one's on your turf, so get back to your day job here and get busy. We're looking for bomb parts, if you can tell the difference between them and auto parts." He waved to an area of the parking lot behind him to the left. "We still have to cover that area and I'd like to get home on time. Wife's cooking her famous lasagna for dinner."

Seamus laughed. "Polish lasagna?"

Q-wicz grinned. "Best kind."

The idea of using kielbasa instead of Italian sausage crossed through Seamus' thoughts. He shook his head. Somehow, searching for bomb parts seemed more appetizing.

"Glad your buddy, what's his name, Napoleon, isn't here. His love of peppermints got me confused at that last scene I worked with him. I didn't know if I was close to another bomb, just residue, or him."

Seamus began walking a grid from a spot Marcinkiewicz had pointed out as a starting place. The man was right about finding auto parts. There were pieces scattered throughout that section of the parking lot. In fact, there appeared to be more debris here than on the opposite side of the lot. The force of the bomb appeared to have been directed this way. He had a good chance of finding bomb parts here, if they existed.

"Heard you guys needed more bodies."

Seamus looked up to see a familiar face, ETU Sergeant Darst.

Darst grinned. "I mean live ones, to help out. Not, you know, more *bodies*."

Seamus shook his head.

"We finished up another crime scene a little while ago and Q-wicz called, said they could use some help."

Seamus chuckled. He didn't know whether or not to tell Darst the real reason Q-wicz wanted assistance.

Eight

After dinner, "Edward" drove to the warehouse and uncovered the Lamborghini. He had one final addition to make—one that hadn't been necessary for his outing a few nights earlier. That had been a successful jaunt. He had gotten the attention of his target, but he hadn't let the man get too close. Guys always want to see the engine, and Edward had yet to deal with that issue.

He started the car and drove it onto a pair of ramps to raise the front end. His craftsman had provided one more goody—make that a set of goodies—to complete the ruse. The VW engine filled maybe half of the engine space under the hood. One look would clearly tell the admirer that the car was a fake.

Edward grabbed the first item from his modeler and slid under the front end of the car with it. He worked it up along the driver's side of the engine and bolted it to the frame. He then did the same for part two, on the passenger's side. Satisfied that both pieces were secure, he returned to the driver's seat and lowered the car from the ramps.

Now, he worked under the hood, placing the final piece across the top of the engine and the tops of both side parts. Lining up specific holes in each side panel with matching holes in the top cowl, he connected the three units with screws.

After 40 minutes of labor, he stepped back and scrutinized his efforts. He closed and opened the hood. He looked at it from numerous angles. He looked for problems that would say, "I'm a fake." Yes, there were minor differences, but only someone who serviced a Lamborghini would notice that this wasn't a real Centenario Roadster engine. The panels even muffled the sound of the VW engine, making it "purr" like the finely-tuned engine that was supposed to be there. Edward wondered if it was too quiet but decided his target was unlikely to notice.

"Edward" smiled. The man—who had killed Edward's betrothed and gotten away with it on technicalities—was about to steal his last car.

To date, the bombs had targeted the "deserving." "Mildred" had risked exposure when she blocked the path of the Good Samaritan with the grocery cart. "Harry" had used a back alley to keep his targets away from others. "Susan" had risked her life to find her prey in no man's land. Their targets were scumbags who had escaped the justice due them. Their previous victims cried out for their punishment. Innocents, however, did not deserve to join them.

But "Edward" faced a dilemma. Self-preservation motivated him as well as doling out justice. He desired to remain among the living, preferably those living in freedom. To do so meant tying up one loose end.

The owner of Jonny Gee's Custom Rods—Jonny Gee himself—was the artisan who had fashioned his fake Lamborghini. He was nationally, if not internationally, known for his craftsmanship. A-list celebrities had sought out his services. He was a go-to guy for those wanting the unique.

He would also be the go-to guy for the police, once they realized they had a fake Lamborghini claiming space in the evidence lot. Edward couldn't blame them for using Jonny and the man was a stand-up guy. He helped the authorities whenever and however he could.

The problem? He knew "Edward's" real identity.

Every sinew in Edward's body resisted what he knew he had to do. Yes, self-preservation was a strong motivator.

This situation, though, could not be traced back to the bomber. What were they calling "him" in the news? The Peppermint Powder Keg? Really? What yahoo came up with that moniker? Even worse, what editor approved it? Maybe he needed to write a manifesto and sign it with a preferred A.K.A.

No. Manifestos had a way of getting traced.

Edward thought about his problem. Jonny's death should be quick and painless. That's the least Edward owed the man whose participation in Edward's scheme was not of his choosing.

He decided to drive the Lamborghini to Jonny's shop to show off the result of the man's hard work— work for which he'd been paid generously. Perhaps while there, inspiration would come to him.

Nine

Over a dozen men and women filed into the conference room at the St. Louis Metropolitan Police Headquarters where the Regional Bomb & Arson Unit maintained their offices and workspace. This morning's meeting was to be the first joint working conference of involved jurisdictions since the first bombing in the north city ghetto. Detectives from SLMPD Districts 2, 4, and 6, the bomb unit, and the FBI task force gathered to compare notes and develop a plan. Detective Marcinkiewicz, as the senior member of the Bomb and Arson Unit, took the lead.

"Okay, folks, let's get this show rolling."

The buzz of conversation died down, and the officers and agents settled into position to take notes.

"I think we've all seen and heard bits and pieces about the three bombings we've had so far . . . and I'm saying 'so far' because I personally don't think he's done. Hopefully, putting those pieces together will begin to show the picture on the face of the puzzle. The first bombing was in District 6, so let's have Brian Welch brief us on what they have."

Welch stood and passed out some papers. "Here's background on the three victims. As you'll see, all three have extensive rap sheets and any number of potential enemies. At this point, we've talked with half a dozen of those potentials and really don't have anything to use. None of them have the smarts or background to stage the explosion we had." He continued with more information on others they had yet to find to interview.

Detective Mike Singer from District 4 came next. He, too, provided background on the two men killed by that bomb. The information sounded like a replay of Welch's descriptions.

Seamus was asked to brief the group on the latest bombing, as the representative of District 2. He had no handout.

"We haven't confirmed any identities on the two victims. There wasn't much left and we're having to rely on DNA. That said, we've been asking around on the street to see who might have disappeared from their usual haunts. One CI gave us a few names, saying they were reportedly behind the recent thefts at that grocery store. A second CI gave us three names, too. One of them matched a name from the first CI's list. The lab hopes that name proves to be a quick match for one of the samples."

Others around the room nodded.

"What's the name? Maybe some of us know him."

The question came from Frank DeLeo. Seamus had

noted that he hadn't been fidgeting in his chair like Seamus had noted on other occasions. The man seemed focused on everything being said.

"Chad Tiffin. His rap sheet appears like déjà vu of the ones you have in front of you. Of note, he recently beat a second-degree murder charge on technicalities." Seamus offered that tidbit of info to see if anyone else came to the conclusion he'd been mulling over.

Seamus was surprised that it was DeLeo—Napoleon—who spoke up.

"Seems this guy might fancy himself a vigilante. Hutchins and Cochran both recently beat cases with long prison terms on technicalities. If Tiffin is confirmed as a victim, that's one guy in each bombing who beat the charges."

Seamus nodded, thinking the agent was finally learning something . . . until he said his next words.

"Maybe we should just let this guy keep doing his job."

From the subtle gestures around the table, it appeared several others agreed, although they were professionals and would never voice that concurrence. It didn't take seeing many criminals back on the streets, freed by liberal judges, to begin to think the system was broken.

Marcinkiewicz said, "Okay, so we might have to consider this the work of a vigilante. He's a smart one. LaToya, up next."

"Or, *she's* a smart one. Since two of the bombings involved purses."

Seamus didn't know this detective, a colleague of Welch's from District 6. His gaze shifted back to Napoleon who had taken a peppermint candy from his pocket, removed its wrap, and popped it into his mouth.

LaToya stood and passed along her handout. "Could be a team, too. A Bonnie and Clyde of bombers, but so-called good guys. Anyway, here's an analysis of the explosive itself. And "smart one" is an understatement. We had to send this to the FBI labs for complete analysis. This stuff is home-brewed. As you know, the manufacturers of explosives have to put a tracer in their compounds that allows us to know where it came from. No such thing in this stuff unless you consider peppermint oil his tracer."

Welch spoke up. "Okay, this chemical stuff is Greek to me. What's all this mean?"

LaToya nodded. "Yeah. So, Alfred Nobel, of the Nobel Prizes fame, was the inventor of dynamite and plastique explosive, which simply means a pliable, moldable compound, kind of like Play-Doh. We're all familiar with C4 and Semtex. Well, Nobel's first compound was Nobel 808 and he used almond oil to make it soft and doughy. In my years of training and work, I've never seen Nobel 808 or even its recipe. It's considered the simplest plastic explosive you could come up with, and this guy, or gal, or team, has found that recipe—with peppermint oil replacing the almond oil. At least, that's what the folks at the FBI labs are saying."

"And this person is making purses with it?"

LaToya shook her head. "Not making them but lining them. Same with the wallet in case two. Like I said, this stuff is like Play-Doh. With a little care, you can roll it out into a sheet and line a purse or stuff a wallet with it. His, or her, detonators are what's truly ingenious, though. We're still trying to figure them out, but we might have a clue."

Seamus watched only a few people perk up, including DeLeo. Was that significant? Did they become alert because one of them was the perp and he wanted to see if the bomb squad got it right? But then, maybe the real bomber wanted to act nonchalant. Seamus decided this was not helpful, but out of habit, he still made a mental note of who did what.

DeLeo pulled out another candy and placed it into his mouth. Seamus noticed that LaToya also watched DeLeo closely. The guy sure liked his peppermints. *Could it really be that simple?* wondered Seamus. Could their perp be sitting in plain sight? Seamus didn't think the guy had the smarts to pull it off. But then, what better way to throw them off the trail than to be so obvious no one could believe he'd be so dumb.

LaToya continued. "The lab found a minuscule trace of ether in one of the samples. What if a small container of liquid ether, say the size of a gelcap, could be ignited by an electrical spark? We're going to test this, but if a small battery—like a watch battery—can produce a spark capable of that, well, think of the small detonators he could produce. Actually, he clearly *did* produce at least one small enough to hide in a wallet.

Nothing could be out of bounds for this perp."

Seamus pondered that concept. The idea was scary. This person could potentially make a bomb out of any common item. He didn't need a cell phone or high-tech device to set off his bombs, unlike those digital countdowns so common on TV.

Ten

"Edward" had learned that LaToya had speculated on his use of ether through "his" usual channel. Remaining among those living *free* required staying a step ahead of the police. She was a smart one, indeed.

At the moment, though, he had a loose end to tie up to finish his day. The previous evening's reconnoiter had shown him that he needed little more than a granny knot to accomplish his goal. Jonny had a penchant for bourbon and Edward had promised him a fifth of the "really good stuff"—as Jonny called it—as a small token of appreciation for his well-done work on the roadster.

With one small addition. Pure grain alcohol had turned this brew from 80-proof to 90-plus. Even Jonny's acclimated liver couldn't process the change quickly enough to prevent a rapid-onset buzz.

"Hey, Jonny. I'm back, as promised."

He held up the bottle of Maker's Mark® as he entered the open work bay of Jonny's shop. He glanced around at the varied projects in different stages of completion. One unusual piece under construction looked like a pod racer from Star Wars, while another appeared, well . . . like . . . uh, like something Edward couldn't describe other than to say it was either futuristic or someone's nightmare.

The man waved from his desk at the far side of the bay. He already had a glass in hand.

Too easy, thought Edward.

"Where's the roadster? Thought maybe you'd bring it back, show it off some more."

Edward shook his head. "Breaking it in slowly. After driving it around some last night, I started to hear a rattle. I need to make sure your work hasn't loosened up a bit with the vibration of being driven. Didn't have time today."

"Ya coulda drove it here. I'd a fixed that in a j-j-jiffy."

Was the man already slurring his words? Maybe the glass in his hand represented more than a first end-of-the-day drink.

"No worries. I got it covered. Here, let me top that off for you."

Edward "cracked" open the seal on the bottle, making sure it mimicked being opened for the first time. He poured a finger's worth of "enhanced" bourbon on top of that remaining in the glass. Jonny pushed an empty glass across his desk toward Edward, who picked it up and inspected it.

"Doesn't look very clean."

Jonny tossed his head to one side. "Prolly not. But the alcohol will shterilize it."

Edward poured a small amount into the glass. "Don't want to be drinking up *your* Mark. It's *your* gift, after all." The man shrugged.

Edward pointed to the futuristic chassis. "What's that one?"

Jonny shrugged again. "Don't know what I'll call it yet. I jus' scribe it as a crosh between *Doctor Who* and *Alien.*"

Edward could see the alien aspects of it. He added a little more to Jonny's glass.

"Whooo-eee. Thasss good shtuff. The maker done make his mark with that batch." He laughed and took another "healthy" swig from the glass.

Within fifteen minutes, Jonny stooped over his desk, laid his head on it, and began to snore. Edward felt relief that Jonny wasn't some "fun drunk" or "angry drunk"—just a let-me-sleep-it-off drunk.

Edward felt a twinge of remorse as he glanced around the garage workshop. He would love to see the final product of *Doctor Who* meets *Alien.* Worse, he hated that he had to snuff out such a creative genius— an innocent man at that.

He wiped down the glass and bottle he had held— no need to leave fingerprints behind— and tossed the contents of the glass before sitting it upside down on the desk. He reached up to a shelf over the desk where a DVD recorder for the garage security system sat. The device was off, but the disk inside showed evidence that it had recorded something. Jonny probably turned it on as he left, to record anything that might happen in his absence. That made sense. Unlike a convenience store, he kept no cash there to entice a thief into a daytime robbery.

Edward debated taking the disk to be sure. He didn't need detectives reviewing it and risk finding his image on it from a previous visit. Instead, he relied on his gut instinct and left the disk in the slot, halfway in, not all the way which would allow the recorder to protect it. With a little luck, the explosion and resulting fire would render it useless.

He wiped the machine to remove potential prints, despite being careful not to leave any trace behind. He checked Jonny. The man remained passed out. He then tipped over the bottle and spilled it across the desk. Again. No trace. No remnant of liquid would remain to let some lab squint determine that the bourbon had been doctored with grain alcohol.

Next, he moved to a propane tank that was hooked up to a soldering torch. Using a rag, he turned on the valve and ignited the torch. He then set the torch into a position where the flame could heat the tank. It wouldn't have to actually cut into the tank to ignite the propane, but he hoped the damage to the tank would make it appear that Jonny had dropped the torch while drunk and had forgotten it before passing out.

He had contemplated using the nearby oxy-acetylene setup for cutting and welding, but logic argued against it on two counts—Jonny was a pro and unlikely to use it with even the slightest alcohol buzz going; and two, the higher temperatures of that system would quickly ignite the gas and leave him less time to get far away. And he wanted to be far away before the extra tanks of gas inside the garage also exploded.

With one quick final glance around the place, he looked at the somnolent man slumped over his desk and said, "I'm sorry." He dashed toward the open bay door and hit the switch to automatically close it. After one more glance back, he exited through the adjacent man door.

He couldn't guess as to how long it would take for the first explosion to occur. The fate of the other tanks was also unknown. The heat of the fire, the rate of acceleration, whether or not the first explosion damaged the tank or its valve—all played a role. The response time of the fire department could also make a difference. All "Edward" knew was that he'd be long gone before any of it.

He smiled as he sat back in the driver's seat. He pulled a peppermint candy wrapper from a small bag and tossed it out the window before starting his car and pulling away. No, he wasn't a litterbug by habit. It was a test. Just how astute were these so-called best-of-the-best detectives?

Eleven

"Be right there."

Seamus looked at the food on his plate and shook his head. Of late, he and dinner had been having an on-again-off-again, long-distance romance. They needed to catch this vigilante so he could enjoy his meals once more.

Vigilante. The term was an Americanism from the early nineteenth century based on the Spanish word *vigilaré*, meaning to keep watch. The more Seamus thought about the bomber the more accurate this term seemed. And that meant he had inside legal info. But the source of that information was a key factor that continued to elude him.

Seamus pondered this factor as he drove to the scene of the latest explosion. The garage of a well-known vehicle customizer had gone up in flames following an explosion. No deaths or injuries had been reported so far.

A uniformed officer let him through the police

cordon and he parked about two blocks away. As he neared the scene on foot, he saw three firemen run from the building. *That's not good*, he thought. Seconds later, another explosion rocked the ground while pieces of the building rocketed skyward. Water continued to be pumped onto the building from a water cannon on the ladder of one nearby truck, as well as through hoses manned by two-man teams. He heard the call go out for another unit to respond.

He frowned. Clearly, his services were not yet needed. Why had he been called?

"O'Connor!"

He turned to see Redmond approaching the scene. Now he understood why he'd been called. Did the man need someone to command and Seamus was the closest at hand? He walked over to the special agent.

"Sir? Why are we here? They don't even have the fire out yet."

"I know. Sorry. I wasn't too happy getting the call either. I think we're going to get called to every explosion and fire in the metro region until we catch this guy. But, we're here. Let's see what we can do."

Together they sought out the battalion commander and waited until he had a moment to brief them.

"You two with the FBI?" asked the commander.

Seamus nodded as the S-A-C answered in the affirmative and introduced them.

"Well, not sure if this will fall in your lap or not. There is a body in there. We can't get to it yet. My guys saw several tanks of gas inside, propane and others. That's why they came running out. Good thing, too. One of those tanks just went off. We need to cool things down or the rest of 'em will explode, too."

"Why'd we get called?" asked Redmond.

The commander pointed. Seamus saw Q-wicz 100 yards away.

"Thanks, Chief."

As they walked toward Q-wicz, Seamus's eye caught the glint of a reflection off something on the ground. He stopped and stooped over to find a peppermint candy wrapper—the same kind favored by Napoleon. Coincidence? He was not a believer in chance.

He picked it up by a small part of one corner.

"Q-wicz, you got an evidence bag?"

The man gave him a look. "Of course. What've you got?" Seamus showed him, and the special agent, and earned one raised eyebrow from the seasoned arson investigator. "Where've I seen them before?"

"Probably every fair, carnival, farmers market, and whatever," replied the agent.

"Well, that, too. But I'm referring to a specific agent we all know and love."

S-A-C Redmond cocked his head to one side. "Hey, you're right. That is the brand DeLeo devours."

Seamus finished sealing the evidence bag. "We should check it for prints. If it has a print that matches his, he'll have some explaining to do. If there are no prints, then it really doesn't help. It's too common a brand. Could be nothing but litter."

Redmond looked at Q-wicz and pointed to the building. "So, why'd you call us here?"

"Sorry, but I'm asking myself that same question. I'm not even on call for the squad and got called here. The story I'm getting is that the first call to come in about this suggested it was the work of our bomber. I get here to find that there's a body inside, they can't retrieve it safely yet, and the first crew on site said it smelled like propane. In fact, nothing here points to our bomber—'cept that candy wrapper you found was for a peppermint. It's a custom auto shop so there's all kinds of flammables here—from solvents and gasoline, to gases for cutting, welding, and soldering. Either somebody didn't like this guy's work, someone had an accident with his propane tank, or somebody is looking to claim some insurance."

Seamus's gut told him there was more to this than any of those explanations. And the candy wrapper? Too convenient. DeLeo made no attempt to hide his love for this candy. Seamus has no idea why the guy ate so many, but Seamus has watched him leave wrappers behind wherever he ate them—for anyone to pick up. Was this wrapper just a red herring, a way for the bomber to implicate one of their own officers and divert the heat from himself . . . or herself? Or was Napoleon truly that clever? To implicate himself and make it appear someone else was framing him.

Twelve

❧ ◆ ◆ ❧

"Heather" glanced in the mirror and added a second coat of mascara to lengthen and darken her lashes. The apples of her cheeks had sufficient blush. Her expert use of concealers and foundation hid every "blemish" of her real skin. She teased her blonde hair to add more volume and then added a deep red shade of lipstick to her lips, pouted, and followed that with a smile. Yes, the lip color topped off a makeup job that any Hollywood pro could be pleased with. *Thank you, Pixiwoo*, she thought as she reflected on the online videos where she'd learned those skills.

Next, she reflected on her outfit. A little padding here. Spanx there. The resulting curves found their prominent display in the skintight top and short skirt. She used both hands to check the bounce of her double-D chest. Perfect. She climbed into the hooker heels she had selected for this outfit and gazed at the completion of her bait. If "Rocky" Hartnett turned a blind eye to this creation, she'd have to give up the title "Mistress of

Disguise"—the flip side to "Edward's" guise as "Master of Disguise."

She needed to hurry now. "Edward" had already parked the Lamborghini at a midtown parking garage near Union Station. He had entered the old station and made his way to a room at the hotel.

Heather emerged from the hotel and walked west along Market Street. If Hartnett was true to form, he'd be at Maggie O'Brien's for drinks. She added a little sway to her hips as she crossed the street to the restaurant. She took only two steps into the place when she saw him. If nothing else, he was indeed a creature of habit—same day of the week, same time, same table.

He saw her and waved. She flashed a smile back and meandered through the midweek crowd toward him. She followed his gaze as he scanned her from head to toe and back to her chest. Yes, her curves would set the trap.

"Hey, beautiful, you are looking m-i-i-ighty fine tonight." He grabbed her and pulled her close. "Wow, I don't know what you're wearing, but you smell as divine as you look," he whispered in her ear.

She felt his hand drift across her right breast. This time she didn't pull away. After all, a man on death row deserved a final meal. Or maybe a little more than a snack, in this case.

"What can I get you to drink?"

"My usual, if you remember what that is," she replied. She ran her hand across his thigh to spring the trap. *However, tonight that meal doesn't come with dessert*, she thought.

Rocky raised his hand to signal the barkeep. "A mimosa for my lady friend!"

Heather rolled her eyes. An Old Fashioned was her go-to drink, but a mimosa would do. She wasn't interested in starting an argument.

Rocky grabbed the drink from the bartender and handed it to her. She took a sip as he leaned into her and whispered in her ear.

"Babe, I got a special treat for you tonight—if you're up for some fun. Wanna take a ride with ol' Rocky?"

She raised her brow in feigned surprise. "Just what kind of fun do you have in mind?"

"Well-l-l, that special ride you asked about. I can make it happen and when we're done we could share some magic together."

She'd heard "it" called all sorts of things, but "magic" was a new one for her personally.

"Really? You have a, you know, that car I've always wanted to ride in?"

He nodded. "Saw one drive by less than an hour ago. And not just any Lamborghini, but a Centenario Roadster. Probably the only one in the entire country. My boys say it's still parked in the garage down the street."

She downed her drink and added some extra bimbo to her character. "Ohh, Rocky, I can't wait. I just know we're gonna have some fun tonight." She gave him a coy smile. "I need to freshen up a bit first. Meet you outside?"

"Gorgeous, I'll be back in less than five. Don't take long because I can't just sit out there waiting for you. Once I have it, we need to get moving."

He looked hungry and eager, but she guessed that hunger had little to do with food. She walked off toward the ladies' room while he paid the tab and disappeared out the front door. She never entered the restroom but waited two minutes before heading toward the curb.

Less than a minute later, she recognized the hum of the Lamborghini's engine and saw the car heading her way. Halfway between the garage exit and the restaurant, where there were no pedestrians at the moment, the driver's side erupted in a ball of flame.

As some people around her scattered and others looked for the cause of the noise, Heather made a beeline east toward the front entrance of the hotel. Mission accomplished, and yet she did not feel at ease.

Thirteen

Seamus felt as if he was operating on autopilot. With only four hours sleep the previous night, his workday seemed a blur of meetings and briefings about the bomber, and then the incident at Jonny Gee's garage. He couldn't remember if he'd eaten lunch or not. Or maybe what he'd eaten was not worth remembering.

Finally home, eager for dinner and an early appointment with his bed, he now held the box of pasta over the boiling water and started to tilt it as the phone rang. He groaned. His gut told him the bomber had struck again. Or maybe he was simply hungry.

"O'Connor."

"Hey, it's Q-wicz. Give you three guesses why I'm calling."

No. This guy, or gal, had a penchant for ruining his dinner. The call definitely had to be about another bombing. Besides, he'd never gotten a call from Q-wicz before.

"You're inviting me over for Polish lasagna. Good

thing you called *before* I started cooking."

"Naw. I finished that off yesterday. But I hope you like peppermint 'cause it smells like a candy factory exploded here."

"Where's here?"

"Next to Union Station. A hundred yards south of Maggie O'Brien's on 20th."

Seamus nodded. "Be there in ten."

At least he'd get dinner. He speed-dialed the restaurant. All of the city's good Irish places were on his phone, although this one was mostly Irish in name only. They had good American fare with names like The Shamrock and St. Paddy's Melt and only a few traditional Irish dishes.

"Molly? It's Seamus O'Connor."

"Hi, Shay. Haven't seen you in a while. You picked a lousy evening to call."

"So I've heard. Look, I'm coming there to work. You think you could have a Paddy Babe's and fries ready for me?"

"Sure. You got it. And we need to talk when you get here."

"Be there in fifteen."

Eleven minutes later, he pulled past the police cordon and parked. He quickly found Q-wicz and Schaeffer. LaToya was nowhere to be seen. As he approached Q-wicz, two ETU vans pulled into the area on the far end of the cordon. Darst climbed down from one and a technician named Griffith drove the other.

"Hey," said Q-wicz in greeting.

Seamus nodded. "You were right about the candy factory. Willie Wonka start a new business here?"

Q-wicz pointed to the remains of a vehicle that the fire department continued to douse. Seamus' jaw dropped as he looked.

"Is that a —"

"Lamborghini? Yeah, and not just any Lamborghini. I had to look it up. A Centenario Roadster, one of their one-offs. Only 10 have been made so far, and only 10 more are scheduled for delivery this year. That's it. And with this one destroyed, the others just got more valuable."

Seamus shook his head in disbelief. The bomber had not only taken another life, he had destroyed one of the most expensive cars in the world.

"I'll be back. I'm gonna check with folks in the restaurant and grab a bite to eat at the same time. When I called to order a sandwich, the manager said she needed to talk with me."

Q-wicz nodded. "Go for it. Looks like we have a few more minutes before we can inspect the car and body. And the medical examiner's van isn't here yet, so we can't do much with the car until the body's removed."

Seamus headed toward the restaurant and saw LaToya drive past the front of Union Station and up to the cordon. He waved. She looked upset.

Wonder what's eating her? he thought.

Inside the restaurant, he found Molly at the bar. As she saw him, she retrieved his food from the back and placed it at an open seat she had reserved near her.

"Thanks, Molly. That looks great and I have a feeling I'm going to be working late tonight."

"On the house. Doesn't look pretty outside, does it?"

Seamus shook his head and proceeded to take his first bite of the overstuffed, smoked corned beef and pepperjack sandwich. After savoring the taste and swallowing, he asked, "So what do you have for me?" He took another bite. His grumbling gut began to calm down.

She leaned closer and spoke softly. "Do you know who was in the car yet?"

He shook his head with his mouth full.

"Well, it might be some guy named Eric Hartnett. Goes by Rocky. He's a regular here and I've been told he makes his living stealing and stripping cars. Not my place to judge and he's never caused trouble here, so . . . You know how it goes."

Seamus swallowed the fries in his mouth and took a swig of iced tea. "So, you think it's him because he was here tonight . . . and now he's not."

She nodded. "Yeah. He was at his usual table and some blonde walked in. He clearly was excited to see her. They talked for a few minutes, and he paid up and headed out the door. The blonde left a couple of minutes later. She couldn't have been outside 30 seconds when the explosion shook this whole place. I ran outside and saw the remains of the car. I also saw the blonde hurrying toward the front doors of the hotel across the street."

Seamus gave her a look. "You think she was involved somehow?"

The manager eased back a bit and answered, "Dunno. It's not like I saw her push a button and the car exploded. But, she was definitely in a hurry to leave the area."

"A hooker?"

She cocked her head to one side. "Maybe. Haven't seen her work here before if she was."

Seamus considered that. Molly and the other long-time workers there would know most of the working girls in that area, with the hotel across the street and two major sports venues within a mile and a half.

"Got video?" He took another bite.

"You know we do. Bring your food and follow me."

Molly sat down at a desk and motioned for him to join her. As he wolfed down the rest of his sandwich and attacked the remaining fries, she found the security footage that started a few minutes before the explosion.

"There." She pointed to a man sitting toward the back. "That's Rocky."

Seamus knew that mug and now he connected the name with it. The man was one of the city's more "prolific" car thieves, and yet, had never been convicted of a crime. There was an ongoing pool to be awarded to the cop who finally caught this guy with enough evidence to convict. The man had also been implicated in more than one vehicular manslaughter case, but again had gone scot-free for a lack of evidence.

Something else about this guy nagged at Seamus.

He would have to look into those files—if the victim proved to be Rocky Hartnett.

"And here comes the blonde through the front door." Molly again pointed to the computer.

The woman made no effort to hide from the security cameras. He followed her movement through the restaurant on different cameras. She seemed glad to be there—until she left Hartnett and headed to the restroom. Her countenance changed, and it seemed clear that she put her 'happy face' back on as she neared the front door to leave. Yes, something disturbed her.

Seamus reversed the video and watched one segment again. He repeated that action three times and finally stopped at one still image that offered him her full face. Where had he seen that face before?

"Edward" watched over the scene as the others began to scan for evidence. Of course, he was not "Edward" at the moment. No. That wouldn't have worked at all. Feeling safe and hidden in plain sight, he went about his routine as the others did theirs.

As his tasks enabled him to approach the vehicle, he wanted to shout out in appreciation of the impeccable job his explosive had done. Every calculation had been correct. "Heather" could have been sitting in the passenger seat and suffered nothing more than blood and tissue spoiling her perfect makeup and tight outfit. Well, that plus a loss of hearing in her left ear.

For Hartnett, however, the story was far different.

The bomb had dispensed its justice.

He glanced about to see if anyone was looking. They all seemed focused on their individual assignments. As he stood next to a lamppost and surveyed the area, he reached up behind the "No Parking" sign strapped to the post. The device he retrieved appeared to be a garage door opener, but the continuous signal it emitted had triggered the bomb as it came within 50 feet. He had no reason to take it other than wanting to use it again. Perhaps he should have left it in place for someone to find and the bomb squad to ponder over its genius, too.

Edward felt his heart race a bit in anticipation. The big reveal had not yet happened. He couldn't wait to see the faces on the others as they learned the Lamborghini was a fake. Perhaps they would appreciate that more than the precision of the explosion.

No, that precision was what made this an amazing case. The car was simply icing on the cake.

Fourteen

Seamus isolated two stills within the video—one of Hartnett and one of the blonde—and had Molly email them to him. He then retrieved them on his phone and made sure both images were available there. He then copied portions of the security video onto a flash drive, thanked Molly for the meal, and headed back outside.

In the distance, he saw the bomb squad, FBI agents, and ETU officers doing their jobs. S-A-C Redmond had also arrived and was talking with Q-wicz.

A number of onlookers stood at the police cordon watching the activity. No doubt they would be denied the part they most hoped to see. The medical examiner's people had erected a walled, portable shelter next to the driver's side of the car in order to prevent the public from viewing the removal of the charred body. As he prepared to work the cordon, looking for witnesses, he knew he would hear complaints from those being denied their viewing of the grotesque. As with public executions, what was it about some people who enjoyed this stuff?

He began to ask for witnesses. Most shook their heads in the negative. A few commented that they'd heard and felt it. Further along the police line, one man in his late twenties raised his hand. He had seen the car exit the parking lot at Union Station and was watching and admiring it when it blew up "like on TV." No, he didn't see the driver and he hadn't paid any attention to other pedestrians because the car was a beautiful thing to behold.

Seamus finished talking with people along that police line and decided to head to the line at the south end of the scene, closest to the exit of the parking lot. He felt surprise to find DeLeo already there and talking with people. He walked up to the agent.

"Hey. Have you found anyone who saw the driver?"

'Napoleon' gave him an imperious look and said, "You just getting here?" The tone in his voice implied that Seamus was a slacker.

Seamus resisted the impulse to roll his eyes and turn away. "No, I didn't just get here. I got here right after Q-wicz called over an hour ago. I've already talked to folks in Maggie O'Brien's and finished working the north line. So, again, any witnesses who saw the driver?"

"No. Just a handful who were admiring the car from a distance when it blew up. Why?"

"I might have a lead on who it was. I'm going to check with the lot attendant."

Glad to leave the contentious agent behind, Seamus began walking south toward the kiosks used by the lot attendants. Whoever had driven the car would have to have paid to get out of the lot. As he walked, his attention was grabbed by a Union Station security guard waving at him from outside his car. He met the man halfway.

"You with the police?" the guard asked.

Seamus identified himself.

"Man, what a waste. That car was gorgeous."

Seamus wasn't surprised that the man was more upset about the car than the driver. He had ceased being shocked about people's materialism and lack of respect for life years ago. Perhaps he had become *too* hardened to that.

"Sorry about the driver, too."

Well, at least the guard tried to redeem himself.

"Did you happen to see the driver?"

The man nodded. "The car came into the lot before our shift change, so I didn't see who drove it in. But, believe you me, I was paying attention to it after I came on duty and saw it. The last thing my employer needs is a car like that to be stolen from this lot, so I paid extra attention to it."

The man rocked gently back and forth, as if waiting to be congratulated on a job well done. Seamus didn't have the heart to tell the guy it might have been stolen after all.

"So, what about the driver?"

"The man walked up to it like he owned it, pulled

out what looked like a remote key fob, opened the door and climbed right in. He started it right up and pulled out. I mean, there was no hesitation, nothing. I figured he was the lucky owner."

Seamus pulled out his phone and retrieved the image of Rocky Hartnett. "This the guy?"

"Yeah, that's him. Hope he enjoyed that car while he could. Guess it proves you can't take it with you, don't it."

Seamus nodded and thanked the man. He followed up by talking with the attendants in the booths. Both confirmed Hartnett as the driver through the image.

As Seamus returned to the scene, his suspicions took center stage. Clearly, Hartnett, a man who had escaped the justice of man's law on multiple occasions, had been targeted. What kind of vigilante would use a $2 million car as bait? The answer seemed obvious. *No* vigilante would do that. The answer to the follow-up question was just as plain. The car had to be a fake.

Every synapse in his brain seemed to fire at once. The explosion at Jonny Gee's garage was no accident. He would need to scrutinize that evidence for any security recordings that survived the fire. Also, Union Station's security footage, and that of the hotel. He needed to trace the movements of that blonde and look for the original driver of the fake Lamborghini.

He ran back to the car and those working around it. Redmond, Q-wicz, LaToya, Schaeffer, Darst, and Griffith all stood there gazing at the damaged vehicle. Redmond turned toward him as he ran up to them.

"O'Connor, you're not going to believe this."

"The car's a fake."

The special agent's face looked crestfallen. "H-how'd you know that?"

"Because the driver was another criminal targeted by the vigilante, and no vigilante in his right mind would use such an expensive car as bait, much less blow it up with his target."

He went on to state he had pretty good confirmation as to who the driver was, the guy's rap sheet, and his multiple escapes from justice, making him a perfect target for the bomber. He stopped short, however, with sharing anything further as he stared at LaToya and wondered what she'd look like as a blonde.

Fifteen

Seamus yawned and fought off the fatigue that seemed intent on overtaking him. He interlaced his fingers, rotated his hands, and stretched them in front of his chest. Then he raised both arms over his head and stretched again. Maybe he needed a quick walk outside to allow the cool, midnight air a chance to waken him. When he had told Molly, he expected a long night's work, he hadn't anticipated the all-nighter this was shaping up to be.

"Ready to work through the next camera?"

Carl, the security office supervisor, sat at the desk with his hand on the mouse. The man had responded to Seamus' request for help with grace and courtesy.

For the past two hours, they had been working through cameras throughout Union Station and the hotel. The blonde had been easy to follow . . . until she wasn't.

After entering the front doors of the hotel, she walked through the lobby and into the old train station which had been refitted with shops, restaurants, and more decades ago. She had wandered through the concourse and back to the hotel where she entered an elevator to ascend to the hotel's rooms. That's where they had lost her. They had checked and double-checked the cameras on each floor and no blonde, just a malfunctioning camera by the third-floor elevator door.

"Hey, this isn't right," said Carl.

"What?" Seamus needed something to make his mind alert again.

"Here's a different camera on the third floor. There's a dark-haired maid coming out of a room with a cart."

Seamus couldn't connect those dots. Housekeepers went in and out of rooms all the time.

"Look at the time stamp. Housekeeping doesn't work that late, and they generally don't take the carts into the rooms."

That woke Seamus up a bit.

"Go back to the time when we lost the blonde."

Carl reversed the replay to find that time stamp. "Sure enough. There she is. Can't see her face."

"That's okay, I've got that. Now go back in time with that camera . . ." He checked his notes. ". . . to just before seven."

Carl complied. "Got her. There she is coming out and heading to the elevator."

They reversed the DVD and watched, hoping to see the woman enter the room. Instead, as they watched in reverse, they saw a bewildering parade of men and women leaving the room, entering the room, and walking backwards toward the elevators. They returned to normal play mode and watched these people again. All of them appeared to be looking for a specific room number, but none knocked on the door before entering. Seamus couldn't tell from the angle of the video, but their actions indicated the door was open for them. None stayed long, but several overlapped where a man entered, then a woman, followed by the woman leaving before the man, or vice versa. He counted five different men and four women. None were the blonde. None offered a face to the camera.

"I don't get this."

"Neither do I . . . and trying to follow each person's actions through these cameras could take a week. Let's check that room."

Five minutes later, they stood outside the room and Carl knocked on the door. No answer.

He used his security keycard to open the door. They walked inside to find . . . nothing. The room appeared unused. The bed linens had not even the wrinkle of someone having sat on it. Carl, however, found and pulled a sheet of paper from the trash can in the bathroom. Together they read:

Thank you again for participating in this psychology class experiment. You will find an envelope with your name on it. Inside will be your next and final set of instructions. Upon completing those instructions, you will receive the payment promised you for participating.

There were no envelopes in the trash can, so either the people had taken them with them, or the "maid" had taken them. If there really were any envelopes. Seamus saw this charade as one big ruse designed to confuse any investigation that got this far.

They returned to the security office and the computer. Seamus wasn't done with the videos.

"Let's keep working backward. Someone had to enter the room and set up the alleged experiment."

A short while later, they found that individual. He had entered the room about an hour before the others. A man of short stature with a bald head except for a fringe of hair around the sides. His clothing seemed that of a caricature of a rich playboy just coming ashore from his yacht, or maybe that of an eccentric psychology professor. Whatever image it was meant to portray, no one today would actually dress that way, would they? Seamus pondered that.

They easily traced the man's footsteps backward in time, from one camera view to the next. In fact, it was almost too easy—as if the man wanted them to notice him. He often smiled directly at the cameras, and of course, his outfit made him stand out in any crowd.

Seamus was not surprised to track him back to the parking lot . . . where he had emerged from a Lamborghini Centenario Roadster.

But who was this guy? Who was the blonde? Something about both individuals seemed, well, familiar. Their statures were about the same as far as height and build. Their ways of walking, while characteristically male and female, held a certain similarity in their actual gait.

"You know," said Carl. "Two things. We never saw the eccentric-looking guy leave the room and we never saw the maid and her cart go into the room, just out of it."

The man was correct. Seamus should have caught that, but he was working on fumes at the moment.

With another review of security footage, they found where the maid entered the room with a cart the evening before. And 30 minutes later, the blonde emerged.

"I'll be."

Seamus had a new thought. "Let's look at all of these people one more time."

Carl queued up the video he had copied to Seamus' flash drive to save time. He played each segment.

"Is it just me or is there something very similar about these people. I mean, look, as they pass that light fixture on the wall. They're all about the same height. Look at the women, the bounce in their chests. Does that look normal to you? Could we be looking at one person disguised as each of these people?"

Carl shrugged. "I see what you mean about height, but three of those women are wearing heels, and the blonde's heels are tall. And I know from my wife that her boobs move differently as she walks depending on which bra she wears. Plus, that guy has a tattoo showing on his wrist just below his sleeve. I don't see that on anyone else. I think these are different people, but that's an interesting thought. Also, the time intervals don't fit and the overlaps don't jibe with that idea."

Seamus sighed. "I'm tired. Thanks to this guy, I've gotten about four hours of sleep in the last two days. Thanks, Carl. You ever think about becoming a policeman? You'd make a great detective."

The man smiled. "I did, for about 30 seconds. I like private security. Better pay, better hours, and a whole lot less hassle. You ever been shot at? Not me. I've had drunks take swings at me, but I've never been shot at. I'll stick with this job, but thanks."

Seamus looked at his watch. *Wow. Is the sun coming up already?* he wondered.

He thanked Carl again for his assistance and observations. Seamus *really* appreciated the observations. He needed some sleep, but he had one more stop—the crime lab. Those folks would be coming in to work shortly . . . if they hadn't already reported to duty.

He found the section he needed—Computer Forensics. His friend, Lynch Cully, and Lynch's mysterious friend, Mike Jorgesmeyer, had tweaked some commercially available facial recognition software for the county's crime lab. Now, the city had it, too.

"Hey, Bess, anybody home?" The door had been unlocked, but Seamus found no one in the room. A door to the actual lab area remained closed.

"Back here."

Seamus nodded and entered the lab.

"Seamus O'Connor, haven't seen you in a month of Sundays. How're you doing?"

"Exhausted at the moment, Bess. It's been an all-nighter working this serial bomber case."

Seamus always found his mood brightened around Bess. The middle-aged black woman had a smile that could light up a city block and a joy that she didn't hesitate to credit to Jesus. And if her smile didn't lighten your load, her gospel singing could get even the most hard-core atheist clapping his hands and swaying with the beat.

"I've been praying about that one, and I'll be praying for you, too, Seamus O'Connor." She walked across the room, poured some coffee into a foam cup and handed it to him. "Fresh brewed. What can I help you with? Seems to me, you should be out there on Olive at HQ with the bomb squad folks."

"Yeah, well, let's keep my visit confidential, okay?" He went on to explain the leadership's concern that the bomber might be one of them.

"Whoa. That wouldn't be good."

"You're telling me. Look, there was a woman involved in two earlier incidents and again in last night's incident, and there's only one woman on the bomb squad. I got a full face shot of the woman last night. Can you compare it to Detective Denise LaToya? She's the last person I'd expect to be involved, but I need to rule her out to satisfy the brass."

"Sure. Let me pull up her photo from personnel and . . ." She extended her hand toward Seamus. ". . . let's compare."

Seamus handed her the flash drive and pointed out the still image of the blonde's face. A moment later, the two faces sat side by side on Bess' large monitor. To Seamus, there was no comparison. LaToya had a natural beauty, while the heavily made-up face of the blonde looked like that of a working girl. And of course, the blonde hair was a stark contrast to LaToya's natural coal black mane.

Two seconds later, Seamus felt as if he'd been punched in the gut. The software gave them a 100% match.

Sixteen

The word was out. Sergeant Denise LaToya was to report to the division commander's office ASAP. Those who knew her were to inform her of the commander's order to report. The fact that this information was broadcast among her peers indicated they had not been able to contact her directly. That already had tongues wagging, along with the urgency implied by the order.

What had she done wrong? Perhaps nothing, but it was the first thing people suspected when the division commander wanted a *tête-à-tête* meeting.

"Edward," however, knew what she'd done wrong. She'd allowed herself to be discovered. She hadn't taken enough precaution as "Heather" and that bulldog detective, Seamus O'Connor, had connected those dots despite "Edward's" and "Heather's" efforts to confuse the identities.

LaToya would have to respond to the call and face her division commander, but Edward had something to do first. That something involved deterring the detectives—and particularly O'Connor—from following the trail. At least that's what "they" hoped to accomplish. With a little luck, O'Connor would get the message and not become a loose end that needed a permanent solution. One innocent man had already died, one innocent too many.

Edward would start with subtle warnings . . . and progress from there.

As he left the Crime Lab, Seamus had heard the call go out for LaToya to meet at the Lt. Colonel's office. He was to be there for the interview as well. He had found the evidence, so he expected to *do* the interview. That was his presumption, provided the big wigs felt no need to upstage him.

He had informed S-A-C Redmond, the Lt. Colonel's office, and his own immediate supervisor that he'd been up all night and needed a few hours of sleep. They had all agreed. The interview was set for one p.m.

He had gone home, pulled down the shades, turned off his phone, set his alarm for 11:30 a.m., and fallen asleep on top of his bed, fully clothed. Unconsciousness had required only that he become horizontal—or maybe just the recognition that he was about to become one with his mattress. As he dragged his groggy body from the bed after hitting "snooze" twice, he realized he couldn't recall actually lying down.

He finished shaving and showering, and dressed in appropriate attire for a meeting at headquarters. As he sat down to eat, he turned his phone back on and was rewarded with the melodious tones of several notifications, both text and phone messages. S-A-C Redmond and Seamus' lieutenant both had urgent messages for him.

He sighed and checked his text messages first—multiple messages from each, 15 to 25 minutes apart. Although not nearly so concise, the essence of each was: *Call me! Now!*

What now? he wondered.

He moved on to his voice mail. One call from Redmond, two from his lieutenant. The special agent's message was to call him before leaving his house. His lieutenant said the same in his first call but offered more details in the second call:

> "O'Connor, I hope you get this before you step out of your house. Brian Welch and his partner both received death threats this morning from the bomber. LaToya still hasn't contacted anyone and we're about to put a BOLO out for her. Be alert and very careful."

He texted both men that he'd gotten the message and would be very alert. He would see S-A-C Redmond shortly and report to his supervisor once the interview with LaToya was finished.

He decided that he should leave a little earlier than he'd planned—just in case—so he wolfed down his food, aided by two cups of coffee. He poured the remainder of the carafe into a travel mug, gathered his materials, and headed toward the door. He was about to open it when his mind said, "Hold on."

What better way to trigger a bomb at his house than to connect it to the opening of his door? He had no idea what might be sitting outside the door waiting for him.

He knelt by the door and opened the mail slot cover. He sniffed the air. Nothing unusual. He looked around the stoop, as far as he could, given the constraints of looking through the mail slot. Nothing. That didn't rule out a bomb. The bomber—LaToya—could have fashioned a bomb to look like a package, or even just a grocery bag hanging from the doorknob.

As he looked about, he noticed his neighbor, Clarence, collecting his trash can. "Clarence! I need your help!"

The man looked about for the source of the voice.

"Over here! My front door! It's Seamus!"

Clarence took a few steps toward the door and nodded his head back and forth. He still looked confused. "Where? I see your door. Where are you?"

"Yelling through the mail slot. I need your help."

The neighbor walked to within ten feet of Seamus' front entrance. "Why are you yelling through the mail slot? Have you fallen and can't get up? Don't you carry your phone with you?"

Good ol' Clarence. Seamus wanted to laugh, but now was not the time. The man started to head up

Seamus' front walk.

"Don't come too close!"

The man stopped and looked as if Seamus was contagious with something.

"Is there anything on or near my door? A package, envelope, bag. Anything. A wire or string attached to the door. Do you smell peppermint?"

Now the guy really gave him a strange look and scratched the side of his head.

"Nope. Looks like it always has, and don't smell anything 'cept the Kramer dog's crap in your yard again."

Seamus rolled his eyes. If only he was around enough to catch the varmint in the act. However, the news he wanted was that his door seemed clear. He yelled once more to Clarence. "Get back to the sidewalk. I'm going to open the door."

Clarence glanced around as if now suspicious that he was being punked, but he did as told and retreated to the sidewalk. Once Seamus saw that he had, he stood, closed his eyes, and opened the door. Nothing, except wondering why in the world he had closed his eyes. Would that have changed anything?

He juggled his things and locked the door. Clarence stood in place on the sidewalk. Seamus walked up to him.

"Thanks. You know I'm on the case of that bomber. Two other detectives got death threats today. I just wanted to make sure there wasn't a bomb on my door. You were there at just the right time to help."

Clarence's eyes bulged wide and he gave a slow nod. "You're welcome. I think." With that he hurried back inside his own home.

Seamus walked to his car and unlocked the door to deposit his stuff inside. As he started to climb in, he stopped. The smell of peppermint was as clear as a clarion alarm sounding off at 150 decibels.

Seventeen

S-A-C Redmond was the first to arrive on the scene at Seamus' home.

"I was almost to the headquarters building when I got the call. You okay?"

"Yeah, I'm fine. Step over by my car. Do you smell it or am I imagining it? I'm seeing things explode in my sleep, so I wouldn't put it past my imagination."

The special agent took only three steps toward the car and shook his head. "Not your imagination. Willy Wonka has been here. Hey, maybe that's what we should call her, the Willy Wonka Bomber."

Seamus shrugged. "Maybe, but the press seems settled on that Peppermint Powder Keg moniker."

Two uniformed officers arrived next and Redmond directed them to cordon off the street. They looked at him like "Who is this guy?" and then at Seamus, whom they recognized as being part of their department. Seamus nodded and the men split up to opposite ends of the street.

Redmond realized what just happened and said, "Sorry, guess I should have identified myself."

"No problem, sir."

The lieutenant pulled up next, followed by the bomb squad van. Seamus noted that it was the other team who had pulled the call, not Q-wicz and Schaeffer. Burlington, Roberts, and Walker were good detectives, even if they weren't the A-team. Seamus pointed to his car.

The three detectives suited up and took on the appearance of sci-fi movie characters. Walker left his visor up, approached the vehicle, and circled it. "The smell is definitely strongest by the driver's door." He lowered his visor and used a mirror on a telescoping rod to look under the car. He pointed. "There she be. About a foot of pipe with something sticking out one end. We'll take a closer look."

Roberts joined Walker with a video camera probe. They both watched the screen as Roberts took a video of the bomb and zoomed in on the thing protruding from the one end. He scrunched his brow and shook his head. "What do you think?" he asked Walker.

The other detective looked as confused as his partner. "Could be a blasting cap, but it's not like anything I've seen. Looks like only one wire coming out of it, but I don't see that wire going anywhere but behind the pipe where we can't visualize it. I don't like this."

Burlington, looking more like the Michelin Man than the others, joined them. Roberts showed him the video and then he eased down onto the pavement next to the car. He reached under the chassis and slowly felt around the bomb. A minute later, he eased the pipe from beneath the car and sat it gingerly on the pavement as he got to his feet. Using their RCV—remotely controlled vehicle, he picked it up and moved it to their containment chamber.

With the device cleared from his car, Seamus walked back to it. Something didn't smell right.

"Hey, Walker. If the explosive is over there, why is the peppermint smell still just as strong?"

He knelt down next to the car and scrutinized the pavement. A small pool of oily fluid sat under where the bomb had been removed. Seamus dipped a finger into it and lifted the sample to his nose. Peppermint oil.

"Guys, there's a pool of peppermint oil there. That's what we're smelling. Does the bomb smell like peppermint?"

Both detectives shrugged. "Didn't get close enough to notice and Carl won't be able to smell it in his suit while the visor is down."

They watched as Burlington manipulated a robotic arm on the disposal unit. Nothing happened. Burlington removed his hood and gloves and then opened the unit. Seamus could see him attempting to suppress whatever he felt at the time, which made Seamus more curious as to what just happened.

Burlington lifted the pipe for all to see. The end where the protrusion had been now just showed an empty hole. The wire was gone, too. The man began to unscrew that end of the device, and it dawned on Seamus that it was coming off much too easily. Everybody circled around Burlington as he removed the threaded end and tipped the pipe. Out came a furled piece of paper, which the bomb squad member uncurled to reveal the word "BOOM!"

Seamus arrived at police headquarters, although a bit later than planned thanks to someone's idea of a joke—or was it really a simple threat from the bomber? LaToya had been unaccounted for all morning. She *could* have placed the fake bomb under his car. He recalled his sense that the bomber went to an extreme to avoid hurting innocent bystanders. To him it seemed fitting that she wouldn't want to injure other members of the "blue" family, but she might want to scare them off.

He entered the division commander's office, its decor simple and unassuming, but its intimidation factor climbed off the charts. He recalled the feeling, having experienced it before when he was on the hunt for a white supremacy group called the Missouri White Alliance. He was glad he wasn't the one being called in.

The lieutenant colonel's secretary greeted him with a smile and nod of her head.

"Sergeant O'Connor, good afternoon. The colonel is with the police chief right now and should be here shortly. Detective LaToya contacted him about an hour ago and will be here in a few minutes. The colonel asked that you have a seat in the conference room. I believe

Special Agent Redmond is there already."

"Thanks. Which conference room?"

The woman pointed. "That way. At the end of the hall."

He nodded and excused himself to head that way. As she had stated, S-A-C Redmond was seated at the table, as was a member of the St. Louis Police Officers Association leadership, J.B. Fletcher. He should have known the union would attend, and since LaToya was a city cop first, and deployed to the city-county joint squad second, her representation by the SLPOA was expected. His only question now was whether she'd have legal representation by the SLPOA, too, or a private attorney.

"Special Agent Redmond . . . John." He nodded to both men.

"The special agent here was telling me about the excitement at your home earlier. Glad it turned out to be nothing."

Seamus looked at the union leader. "I guess—if you call threatening a police officer and requiring a response by the bomb squad nothing."

The man bobbed his head in acquiescence. "You know what I mean. It could have been—"

They were interrupted by the entrance of the division commander, Lt. Colonel William Cooper. He acknowledged them all and sat down.

"Detective LaToya and her counsel are here. Before we start, I want to make it clear that O'Connor will start off with his findings and then we'll let LaToya respond. I'll ask questions after that. Any issues with that approach?"

Nobody raised any questions, so the colonel went to the door and invited the detective and her lawyers into the conference room.

Seamus noted that Denise LaToya appeared in distress. The signs were subtle—intermittent hand wringing, the occasional deep breath, a look of concern in her eyes. These were not typical of the woman he knew, a woman who held her own among the men of the bomb squad as well as those she served with in the military.

"Detective, counselors, before Sergeant O'Connor begins, I want you to understand that this meeting is for fact finding and to give you a chance to respond. There is no one here from the district attorney's office. You have not been charged with anything, but how you respond here will determine what steps might be taken in the immediate future."

"Is Detective LaToya under arrest?" asked one of the lawyers, a woman Seamus had never seen before.

The other lawyer was an attorney well known for his work with the SLPOA in defending police officers. He sat there as if he'd been through this before. The woman, however, seemed defensive before Seamus had said a single word. By her attire, he would guess her to be a defense attorney privately obtained by the detective. That in itself said something about LaToya— she was worried.

Seamus glanced at the colonel and saw that he was

already annoyed by this attorney.

"Ms. Simpson, as I stated, Detective LaToya has not been charged with a crime, so, no, she is not under arrest. May we start?"

The lawyer nodded and appeared to calm down, but LaToya's stress level seemed to increase.

At the colonel's okay, Seamus began to present his case. Three of the four fatal bombings appeared to involve a female perpetrator. Of the single incident that reportedly involved a man, the detective was on the scene within minutes and self-admitted to being at Laclede's Landing at the time. Her story about being there with family to eat could not be corroborated by anyone else. She had the expertise to create the explosive as well as the elaborate bombs. Seamus continued.

"However, all of the evidence in the first three cases is purely circumstantial. There is nothing to tie Detective LaToya directly to those events. The last case, however, is different. This case involved a woman named Heather. We have multiple witnesses to Heather's meeting with the victim and disappearance as soon as the explosion occurred." He went on to explain his actions of the previous night, tracing Heather at the hotel and culminating with facial recognition confirming that Heather was, in fact, Denise LaToya.

Seamus saw the thin facade of calm on LaToya begin to crack at the initial mention of Heather. By the time he had laid out the photographs and screen grab of the facial recognition program, she was sobbing. That stunned Seamus. He had seen her work under extreme pressure and in life-threatening situations without a hint of emotion. Now, she cried.

She started to say something, but the female lawyer stopped her and began whispering frantically into her client's ear. The union lawyer leaned in to hear the conversation. Seamus could only pick up a stray word or two.

LaToya kept shaking her head. She finally turned away from the lawyers and faced Seamus.

"Yes, I-I was Heather, b-but I didn't do the bombing, any of the bombings. The guy goes by the name Edward and he has a bomb at my folks' house. He th-threatened to kill my parents and brother if I didn't help him with Hartnett."

She seemed to collapse emotionally. "I've spent hours looking for the explosive at their house. I've checked their cars. I've even been to Dad's workplace. This guy can disguise his plastique as anything, and he doesn't always use peppermint oil. That's just his signature right now . . . for these vigilante cases."

"Why didn't you move your family out to a safe place?" asked the colonel. "You could have come to us then."

She shook her head. "I tried that. They went to my mom's sister's house. The next message I got from Edward included the address where they'd gone and threatened my aunt, uncle, and cousins, too. To make his point, he blew up a trash receptacle just a hundred yards from the house. That was the first explosion we investigated. He told me to expect peppermint as his calling card."

Seamus could see the fear in her eyes. Was her divulging of this information dooming her family?

"Denise, does your family know about the danger?"

She nodded. "Yes. Of course. There's no way I'd keep that from them."

Seamus looked at the colonel. "Sir, if they confirm this we need to get them all to a secure place ASAP, including the aunt's family." The commander nodded.

"Who is this Edward?" asked S-A-C Redmond. The colonel gave him a look.

LaToya shook her head. "If I knew that, none of this would have happened. He contacted me through a variety of methods, almost like he'd learned tradecraft in the CIA."

Something else struck Seamus about this whole thing. Why did he need help with Hartnett? And why the expense involved in taking out that man?

"Why did he recruit you for this one bombing? I mean, think about it. He clearly presented himself as a woman on two other occasions. I suspect he arranged to kill or set up the explosion at Jonny Gee's garage to cover up the man's work on the fake Lamborghini."

LaToya looked contemplative and didn't answer right away. "I-I don't know. It does seem like a lot of expense to kill one man. Maybe the others were practice, in a gruesome sense." She appeared thoughtful again. "Or maybe, he needed a real female for this one. I had to cozy up to Hartnett, play the easy woman who promised him a good time if he proved his skill by stealing a Lamborghini and giving her a ride."

Seamus shook his head. "That last part makes sense, but the others? No. They were a smoke screen, a way to make this look like a vigilante killer when he was really after Hartnett all along."

"That all makes sense to me," said the colonel.

Over a brief recess, it took one call by Seamus to confirm LaToya's story about her family, and a second, by the colonel, to set up protection. After the break, the colonel and Seamus had more questions for the detective and only the union attorney remained with her. The answers added little more to their investigation, but Seamus knew that Hartnett was the key to solving these crimes.

Eighteen

Edward had his ways of learning what had transpired in the meeting between LaToya and the others, but to act on such information would give too much away. He had to act as if he'd had no knowledge of the meeting.

Yet, he realized now that he'd made one critical mistake. He had acted too swiftly in his zeal to claim revenge on Hartnett. Patience would have proven to be a better move. The rapid sequence of test explosions followed by the vigilante actions had moved the FBI to take over and form the task force. He should have known that O'Connor would get called up. And then to plan two incidents within O'Connor's own turf, District 2? What had he been thinking? Had he been underestimating O'Connor?

Perhaps. Now he had to deal with the fallout.

He put himself in O'Connor's shoes. How would the man think? What would be his next move?

As he paced, his thoughts raced. The detective's

next move became clear—to research Hartnett and the various failed cases against the man. At one point, Edward wondered if going to the expense of the fake Lamborghini had also been a mistake. It did, after all, make that case stand out from the others. And yet, Hartnett was a man who loved a challenge and thought with his loins. The ruse with LaToya's "Heather" was the only fail-safe way to get to the man.

Edward faced a dilemma. Option one—to develop a plan with a new target that would make the Hartnett case seem like a decoy. The finances weren't there to create as elaborate a device as that Lamborghini, so it would have to be a target of greater "importance." But who?

Option two—lay low for a while and continue the vigilante course. By adding greater numbers, the importance of Hartnett would diminish. Maybe, too, the added time would give him the opportunity to find a suitable target for option one.

And yet, neither option really seemed viable.

He walked over to a nearby window and stared into the distance. Edward wasn't a killer at heart. Neither were "Mildred," "Harry," or "Susan." Or were they—make that, was he? Each character had killed. Was there a part of "Edward"—or the others—that enjoyed the killing? Was "he" simply justifying some deeper aspect of "his" real self by claiming to exact the justice that the system failed to produce? Maybe the role of judge and executioner was a good fit.

No matter. To pursue both of those options

required staying in the land of the free. The basic instinct of self-preservation remained strong, and that meant he had only one real choice.

Option three—remove the man who threatened to take away his freedom.

Following the meeting with LaToya, Seamus returned to the office to complete several days' worth of neglected paperwork. Paperwork was the bane of his existence, like it was with so many "jobs." His on-again, off-again girlfriend, Sarah Wade, MD, had completed her year as chief resident in the Emergency Department at Barnes Hospital and now worked as an attending physician at another department. She had the luxury of a scribe, someone who followed her while seeing patients and handled all the paperwork. He knew he shouldn't be jealous, but he was.

He stared at the last case he needed to complete, hoping it would somehow take care of itself. He recognized that it wasn't that specific case or the paperwork in general that made his eyes glaze over, but simply the fatigue. He needed to go home, eat a real meal—preferably cooked by someone else, because he was too tired—and go to bed. His perspective on everything would improve with some much-needed rest.

After picking up some food from his favorite Italian place on The Hill—St. Louis' Italian neighborhood, he returned to his home in the adjacent

Shaw neighborhood. He found a parking place on the street a few homes down from his own. As he approached his place, a FedEx truck pulled up in front of his home and double-parked as the driver jumped from his cab and carried a small package to his door. The man saw and recognized him as he turned to return to the truck.

Seamus became wary in an instant but not because of the driver' actions. The same guy had been delivering to his house for over two years.

"Hey, Gary," said Seamus. " Thanks, but I'm not expecting any packages. Where's that from?"

There was an edge in his voice that did not go unnoticed by the driver.

"Sorry, Sergeant, didn't really pay attention to that. It's my last package of the day and had to be delivered by 6 p.m. Fifteen minutes to spare. Instructions also said to keep it in the shade. Must be chocolate or candy or something by the minty smell of it. Enjoy."

Seamus' fatigue dissolved away. He had more questions for Gary, but the man rushed to his truck and sped away before Seamus could stop him. Seamus pulled his phone from his pocket and speed-dialed dispatch. Seconds later, a call went out to the bomb squad. They would not be pleased to respond to his home for the second time that day, but he had no choice. The driver's description of the package smelling minty was all the prompting he needed to call them into action.

Then it hit him. Why 6 p.m.?

He glanced at his watch and saw that it was eight minutes before the hour. Eight minutes, and that package sat next to his front door. Did he have just eight minutes until the front of his home disappeared in a blast that would shake the petals off the flowers at the nearby Missouri Botanical Gardens?

No way. He'd spent too much time lovingly restoring the old home. The package hadn't exploded with Gary's carrying it to the front door. It wasn't likely to do so if he carried it to a safer spot. He had seven minutes.

But where? The sidewalk was but 20 feet from the front of his house, and his neighbor's car was parked there. He looked both ways along the street. Four doors down, in the direction away from his own car, he saw an open section in the street with no cars parked on either side for at least 30 feet. That in itself was a miracle.

He saw a car coming down the street. He raced the car to the open area on the street. He managed to set the package down and waved the car to a stop. The driver laid on the horn, not happy at being stopped and deprived of a prime parking spot along the usually crowded street.

Seamus flashed his badge as the driver powered down his window. Seamus knew everyone who lived on the street. This person was a stranger.

"I'm here to visit—"

"You need to back up and turn around if you can. I think it's a bomb and the bomb squad is on the way. You need to clear the area."

The driver looked confused. "I . . . I . . ." He glanced into his rear-view mirror. "Okay."

As the man began to back up, Seamus heard a car behind him. He turned, prepared to shoo away another driver but saw that it was a police car that now blocked traffic from that end of the street. He heard sirens approaching from the north, as he glanced at his watch again: 5:59 p.m.

Somebody's clock was off. Ten seconds later, the blast knocked Seamus off his feet.

Nineteen

Seamus sat on the steps leading from the sidewalk to his front walkway. He waved off the paramedic he saw coming his way. He felt fine, other than some ringing in both ears. The paramedic persisted.

Seamus shook his head as the young woman approached. "I'm good. Just knocked me on my butt, not my head."

She smiled. "Well, O'Connor, from what your lieutenant over there says, it might have been better the other way around. He told me to check you out, and if you refused, to ask for a 96-hour psychiatric hold. They told me you decided to carry the bomb to the middle of the street rather than wait for the bomb squad."

He used his thumb to point over his shoulder at his house. "Yeah. If I'd waited, I would have a big hole in the front of my house."

"Good point. Still, let me give you a quick once-over and we can make the brass happy. Okay?"

He nodded and sat still as she checked his vital

signs; his ears, eyes, and head; and did a short neuro check. He crossed his eyes as she asked him to follow her finger with them.

"Cute. Why do you guys always do that? I could retire early if I had ten dollars for everyone who did that to me."

He smiled. "I'll put in a good word for you."

"Thanks." She closed the top on her aide bag. "If you want to go to the ER to get—"

"No thanks. I know the drill and I'm fine, like I said."

"Yes, you do, and you know I have to put you down as a refusal of service."

"No problem."

The ringing had diminished, so he stood and followed her back to the lieutenant. He grinned as the paramedic reported to his boss.

"Stubborn as ever, but he checks out okay."

"Thanks, Cheryl. Maybe it knocked some sense into him."

She laughed and headed back to her rig.

"Hey, I landed on my butt, not my head."

"Exactly. Like I said," replied the lieutenant. "By the way, Walker says it was actually a fairly small charge. He thinks it might have knocked your door off its hinges but wouldn't have damaged much more. Had it gone off as you carried it, however? It would have been *beannacht go deo* for one Irish detective."

Goodbye forever. The lieutenant surprised him that he knew more than "pass the Guinness" in Irish. He was correct, however, about Seamus' fate had he been wrong about the bomb and the timing.

"You sure you want to stay here tonight? This guy Edward, or whatever his real name is, clearly knows where you live."

That concern had already crossed Seamus' mind. Did he stay to protect his "castle?" Or, should he leave for a hotel? A change in scenery hadn't seemed to work for LaToya's family. Either way, he was going to have trouble sleeping—worrying about himself and about his home—and that's not what he needed.

"Yeah. I think I'd rather stay here and defend my home if it comes down to that. Besides, I'm convinced this was just another warning, a shot across the bow. The fake bomb this morning didn't work, so he escalated it a little."

"Maybe, but he had to have known that the fake wasn't going to work. He would have had to put this package in the FedEx system no later than yesterday to get it here by tonight."

That thought, too, was not new to Seamus. In fact, he would be contacting FedEx in the morning to find out where, when, and hopefully, who shipped the package. He didn't like the thought that LaToya knew where he lived and had been free from scrutiny during the time the package had been shipped. Had she omitted something in their talk?

But who else on the squad knew where he lived? The three members who responded today now had that information, but he didn't think any of them knew his address previously. Q-wicz had been to his house for a cookout once before. Q-wicz as the mysterious Edward? Surely LaToya would have recognized something in Edward's voice that pointed to Q-wicz if he was the bomber. Schaeffer? Not likely. Who else could be a candidate?

Seamus glanced across the crime scene and watched the three bomb squad members as they combed the area. Members of the ETU assisted. He debated stepping in to help but knew he couldn't. He was the target of the bomb. Any evidence he touched risked being thrown out of court. As he observed, Sergeant Darst of the ETU waved him over. Burlington had joined him.

As Seamus approached he saw the detectives examining a large fragment of the package. He was surprised that so much of it remained intact.

Burlington asked him, "How did you grab the package when you carried it to the street?"

"Like this." He demonstrated, having placed both hands flat against the sides and lifting it. He had mimicked the way Gary, the FedEx driver, had carried it.

"Was the shipping label facing you, or sideways?"

Seamus had to think a moment. "Uh. Facing . . . away from me. Upside down for me to read it."

"So, not sideways in either case."

Seamus nodded. "Why?"

"You're luckier than we'd figured before. See this?"

Darst pointed to some sort of panel on the remnant

of the package.

"Small solar panel. We haven't found any battery fragments yet, so it probably charged the timing mechanism."

Seamus recalled what Gary had said. "The driver said he had instructions to place it in the shade."

Burlington nodded. "Maybe the bomber expected you to react and move it away from your house, where it would have ended up in the late afternoon sun. But the way you carried it, your hand covered the panel and prevented it from charging the timer. I suspect we'll find there wasn't any clock set to 6 p.m., just a timer. If you had picked it up any other way . . ."

The detective didn't have to finish his sentence. But Seamus now understood the need to meet a time deadline.

"Guys, this time of year, the evening sun hits my stoop shortly after 6 p.m."

Twenty

Seamus awoke with his alarm that morning. He had been wrong about losing sleep. His fatigue had overcome his worry within an hour after finishing his rewarmed, take-out meal. The bomber could have taken his house down around him during the night and he wouldn't have wakened.

Following breakfast, he went to work to discover that his colleagues had wasted no time in festooning his desk with "trash talk" about his escapade of the previous night. One printout showed a suit of armor for sale. Others held memes about finding evidence at bomb scenes—scenes with arrows pointing here, there, way over that way, back behind you, and so on. He had seen most of those before. He had to laugh at one that showed him wearing a big, inflatable bumper ball at a bomb squad recruiting meeting. Someone had taken some time on that one.

He smiled as he cleared his desk. Nothing like cop humor, except maybe emergency room humor. Sarah would appreciate these gibes, so he refrained from tossing them into the recycling bin.

His first order of business? To hunt down the cases involving Rocky Hartnett. He remained convinced that the man was the key to finding "Edward."

He signed onto his computer and began his search at Case.net through the Missouri government website. He started here because the database covered *all* state court cases, not just those within the city or metro area. He entered the man's first and last names as search criteria. The man was the literal career criminal, with over 50 cases entered against the man—from speeding tickets to stealing. However, what amazed Seamus was that all 14 of the felony stealing charges against the guy had somehow been dropped and the cases dismissed. These had to be the auto thefts he'd heard mentioned.

He followed this by working through the REJIS (Regional Justice Information Service) and Crime Matrix databases. He made note of the various jurisdictions involved in these cases and began networking with the various detectives on those cases.

"Hardy."

"Detective Hardy, thanks for taking my call so quickly. This is Seamus O'Connor. We met at an information exchange meeting in St. Peters a few months ago."

"Yeah, I remember. What can I do for you, O'Connor?"

"Rocky Hartnett. Ring a bell?"

Seamus heard a grunt on the other end of the line.

"Yeah, more like a klaxon. Heard the scumbag took his last ride."

"Yep. What can you tell me about him?"

The detective seemed to need no notes as he launched into the details of three cases his department had brought against Hartnett.

"So, what happened to those cases?"

"All dismissed. In one case, the evidence was determined to be circumstantial. In another, an ex-girlfriend gave him an alibi. In the third, some crucial DNA evidence got lost. That last one was the hardest for me. The guy killed a young woman who was seven months pregnant. She and her boyfriend were to be married a few weeks later. That was a tough one. In fact, if I remember correctly, the fiancé was a police officer somewhere in the area. I'd have to pull the records and see if we have a name for him."

Seamus became more attentive. One of their own? Motive?

"Would you check and let me know?"

"Sure."

"Thanks."

They signed off and Seamus moved to the next department, and then the next one on his list. Each detective had no trouble recalling Rocky Hartnett and his cases. In two others, vehicular manslaughter was involved. One was a young man just a month shy of his wedding. His fiancée was in the military. The other involved a young mother of two, but the husband had moved to Arizona shortly after the accident.

By the end of the day, Seamus had talked with detectives in every police department where Hartnett had operated. The more he learned about this man, the happier he was that the man was off the streets. Permanently. The more he thought about this man, the more convinced he became that he now understood "Edward's" motive—the death of his pregnant fiancée. His gut told him he was within reach of identifying the bomber.

Twenty-One

The next morning found Seamus meeting at the FBI field office with the joint task force. He had hoped Detective Hardy would call him back with a name prior to the meeting, but that hadn't happened. He would now have only conjecture to present to his peers.

He scanned the conference room for an empty seat. Welch was seated between two agents, with Q-wicz flanking the agent seated farthest away from the door. Schaeffer was on the other side with two more agents and AJ Darst. AJ waved at him and pointed to the empty chair next to him.

As Seamus claimed that space, S-A-C Redmond opened the meeting.

"Good morning. Let's get started. Detective Marcinkiewicz, you have an update for us."

Q-wicz nodded. "A follow-up on the Jonny Gee garage explosion and fire. Even though it looked like an accidental explosion at first glance, the lab found traces of nearly pure ethanol on the remains of a table where the deceased was found and in a partially melted bottle. And the ME reported a blood alcohol level at five times the legal limit."

No one around the table commented. They all had seen too many people with such levels—many of them driving at the time.

"We canvassed Gee's employees and friends and they all acknowledged that the man was a major league drinker. But, they all agreed that he drank cheap stuff and nothing nearly as potent as what was found in the bottle. In fact, the bottle had the markings of Maker's Mark®, pun intended, but the alcohol traces were over 90-proof—evidence the bourbon had been spiked. The folks we interviewed also agreed that the man would never have left his propane torch on. He had a ritual of making sure everything was turned off before taking that first drink of the evening. So, when we put this together with the fake Lamborghini, we believe our bomber was responsible for this death as well."

That was a conclusion that Seamus had already made, but now he had supporting evidence. His phone vibrated in his pocket. Maybe Detective Hardy was getting back to him. He retrieved his phone and opened the home screen. Nope. Just a text message from another department. They had found the case files on another of Hartnett's alleged manslaughter incidents. They'd get back with him by the end of the day.

AJ Darst leaned over to him. "Hey, I'm getting another cup of coffee. Need some?"

As Seamus was about to answer in the negative,

the ETU sergeant stood and knocked Seamus' phone to the floor.

"Sorry, let me get that."

Darst knelt on the floor and poked his head under the table. A few seconds later, he rose up and handed Seamus his phone. "Here. Sorry." He left to refill his coffee cup and returned a minute later, as one of the FBI agents presented their data on past and present military demolition folks who might live in the area. Half a dozen men fit their search criteria, but none remained a person of interest after being interviewed.

By the end of the meeting, little new information had been presented. They were no further along in identifying "Edward" than they had been before the conference. Detective Hardy had not come through in time.

As the others left the room, Seamus stayed behind. He wished to brief S-A-C Redmond privately on what he'd found. He would present his information to the rest of the task force when he had a name and had tied up some other loose ends.

Fifteen minutes later, Seamus left the conference room and walked down the hall toward the elevators. Halfway there, a short, balding man carrying a tall stack of papers bumped into him. A portion of the stack flew to the floor.

"Oops. Sorry. I got distracted and didn't see you."

Seamus helped pick up the papers. He saw nothing unusual about the man and he wore the appropriate identification on a lanyard around his neck.

"No problem. Here you go." Seamus placed the short pile of papers he had collected on top of the man's stack.

He proceeded to the elevator and pushed the button. At that moment, his phone rang. He reached into his pocket and retrieved it. It wasn't ringing. The screen was blank. His usual ringtone sounded again. He reached into his other pocket and found a phone. His phone? He looked at both. They seemed identical.

As he answered the one phone, he pressed the power button on the other.

"O'Connor, it's Hardy. Hey, got that name for you. Aaron Darst. He was with county police at the time."

Seamus heard the message, but his eyes were glued to the other phone, which now offered a digital countdown. 20 . . . 19 . . . 18 . . .

The scent of peppermint hit him.

"Bomb! Everyone, get away!"

He held the phone at arm's reach and realized that would be useless. Where? He had 15 seconds and he had no reason to believe this was a fake.

Redmond raced around the corner. "This way!"

Seamus took off in a sprint and found Redmond holding the door to the emergency stairwell. As they both entered it, Redmond called out, "Clear the stairwell! Bomb! Clear the stairwell!"

Seamus could hear doors slamming shut above and below them.

"Drop it! Down the center!" yelled Redmond.

10 . . . 9 . . .

Seamus understood the man's assessment of the situation in an instant. The stairwell was reinforced concrete designed to withstand tornadoes and earthquakes. It offered the best chance of withstanding an explosion based on the size of the charge that could fill a smartphone. He looked over the handrail and found the clearest path for dropping the phone. He didn't want it to deflect off a handrail and end up on the steps.

7 ... 6 ...

He dropped the phone and then dove for the floor, covering his ears with his hands. S-A-C Redmond had already done the same.

BOOM! The stairwell vibrated for a second, a wave of high air pressure filled his nose, and the doors throughout the stairwell rattled.

Twenty-Two

Sergeant AJ Darst was apprehended by the FBI before he could drive his ETU van from the field office's parking lot. As the agents escorted him, handcuffed, back into the building and to an interrogation room, Seamus thought he looked puzzled. In fact, Seamus was also puzzled.

The man had the opportunity to plant the fake phone when he retrieved Seamus' phone from under the table. Yet, if so, why had he taken so long to leave the premises? It didn't make sense. If Seamus had been the bomber and had planted the phone bomb on someone, he would have cleared that building and sped from the scene as quickly as possible.

But Darst appeared as if he knew nothing about it.

S-A-C Redmond stormed into the room ahead of Seamus. The man was livid. This attack hit home for him and he wanted Darst's head on a platter.

"Sergeant Darst, you are under arrest for the serial bombings, the murders of eight people, and various federal terrorist charges, including the attack on this federal facility."

Seamus noted the man still looked confused.

"I-I didn't do any of this. I'm on your side here."

Redmond laughed. How many times had each of them heard that?

"Seriously. I didn't do these things." The man seemed to be getting angry now.

Seamus gave him a nutshell version of his information on Rocky Hartnett and finished by saying, "Detective Hardy called me just as I discovered the bomb in my pocket. It was you, Aaron Darst, whose pregnant fiancée was allegedly killed by Hartnett."

The man looked stunned and didn't say a word in reply. After a moment, he asked, "Will one of you get my wallet from my back, left pants pocket?"

Seamus complied.

"Will you check my driver's license?"

Seamus opened the wallet to find the license made out to *Albert* James Darst.

"Aaron Darst was my brother. He was a county patrol officer and he died in Afghanistan a year after his fiancée was killed. I'm not your guy. I'm not this Edward person."

AJ Darst was held for 23 hours while his story was investigated. At that point, nothing was found to prove that he was the bomber. He had solid alibis for all of the bombings and his property held no traces of explosives—only the hobby he was known for, exotic snakes.

Seamus cinched on his protective vest and joined the FBI team that was about to serve a warrant on the real bomber. Another team had a warrant for a storage garage rented by this person. Their bomb-sniffing dog had already become agitated at the door to the garage, a sure sign they were about to find what they expected inside—a bomb-making lab.

The lead agent knocked on the home's door and announced their presence. No answer. Seconds later a battering ram took down the door and the agents stormed inside. Seamus was in the middle of the pack.

The first agents took to the stairs and cleared the second floor. Seamus joined those combing the first floor. No one home, so far, but Seamus noticed the door to the basement being ajar. He headed down.

The bomber sat in a chair and appeared to be asleep. Seamus spotted an empty glass and pill bottle on the floor. He suspected this sleep was one of a final nature. He checked for a pulse but found none.

The other department had come through early that morning. The other vehicular manslaughter case had involved an Edward Wells . . . and his military fiancée was none other than Warrant Officer Denise LaToya.

Thank you . . .

I hope you enjoyed *Ten Seconds 'til.* Please consider writing a review. They are crucial to Indie authors such as myself. It doesn't have to be lengthy. Just a couple of sentences will do. You can post it wherever you bought the book. Thank you.

Also, if you'd like to stay informed about my new books, book signings, and more, please sign up for my newsletter. You can do that at my website. As my thank-you for signing up, I'll give you my eBook, *And Then One Day*, a prequel to the MedAir Series. The story tells how the main characters—Lynch Cully and Amy Gibbs, RN—met. Of course, Seamus O'Connor is also part of that story.

And did you know you can purchase signed copies of my paperbacks at my website? With shipping included in the price—U.S. only, international shipping is extra—ordering them directly from me is typically cheaper than ordering them online.

ACKNOWLEDGMENTS

For this short novella, the list of acknowledgments is brief:

My thanks and gratitude, as always, to my loving and talented wife, Paula, for her valuable assistance, whether it be proofreading skills, general help, or all-around encouragement. Also, thanks to Lenda Selph for your invaluable proofreading skills and suggestions on the story.

Here's a special shout-out to Joe Marcinkiewicz of the St. Louis Regional Bomb & Arson Unit. With such a defining name as his, how could I not make him a character—even if somewhat embellished—in this book?

And finally, a hardy thank-you to Sgt. Terry Kenniston of the Maryland Heights Police Department for your input into the police aspects of the story.

ABOUT THE AUTHOR

Braxton can't lay claim to wanting to be a writer all his life, although his mother and seventh grade English teacher were convinced he had what it would take. A bachelor's degree in Bio-Medical Engineering led to medical school and a residency in Emergency Medicine. He served for a decade in the U.S. Army Medical Corps with tours such as the Chief, Emergency Medical Services at Fort Campbell, KY, and as a research Flight Surgeon at Fort Rucker, AL. Who had time to write?

By the 1990s, as a civilian, his professional and family life had settled down, somewhat, and his mother once again took up her mantra, "Write a book. You're a good writer." In 1997, a Valentine's Day writing contest convinced him that maybe he could write fiction. He spent the next fifteen years learning the craft of writing.

Now, 20+ years after that first hesitant start, he has sixteen novels published, as well as non-fiction books and a children's book, and can't find enough time to write. As a Christian, he writes "true-life" Christian fiction (suspense and thrillers) that many call "cutting edge," as he's not afraid to take on such issues as human trafficking, racism, and more. His characters are real-life as well, with all their flaws and blemishes. As such, his books are never likely to gain acceptance by the Christian Bookseller Association. But then, he never intended to tell stories just to the choir.

Books by Braxton DeGarmo:

Still Here Series:

The End Begins - 1
The Shaking - 2
The Beasts – 3
The Trumpets – 4
The Mark - 5

Non-fiction Study Guides:

Still Here! Surviving the End Times
Still Here! The Apocalypse is Now
Still Here! Countdown Revelation

MedAir Series:

Looks that Deceive – 1
Rescued and Remembered – 2
The Silenced Shooter – 3
Wrongfully Removed – 4
A Zealot's Destiny – 5
Kidnapped Nation - 6
The Khmer Connection - 7
Resurrected Trouble - 8

Seamus O'Connor Thrillers:

The Militant Genome
Ten Seconds 'Til

Other Books:

Indebted

Children's Books:

The Toucan Who Can Can-can

www.ingramcontent.com/pod-product-compliance
Lightning Source LLC
Chambersburg PA
CBHW060747210726
48292CB00015B/2819